PADMINI

...ula Behari is an award-winning Hindi writer. Since 1977, she has ...n several short stories, novels and plays for the theatre, radio and ...sion. Her work has also appeared in several leading publications ... as the *Hindustan, Saptahik Hindustan, Dharmayug, Saarika* and *Kadambini*, besides being translated into other Indian languages. ... most recent among her many awards is the Rajasthan Sahitya ...demi's Meera Puraskar for 2008–09. She spends her time ...ween Jaipur, Chicago and San Francisco.

...tranand Kukreti is a freelance writer, translator and journalist who ... translated several short stories and poems, including one by former ...me Minister Atal Bihari Vajpayee. He has also translated a book on ...st Amrita Sher-Gil from Hindi to English, besides translating into ...di C.K. Prahalad's bestseller *The Fortune at the Bottom of the* ...mid. At present, he is working on a Hindi-English dictionary.

PADMINI

THE SPIRITED QUEEN OF CHITTOR

MRIDULA BEHARI

TRANSLATED BY MITRANAND KUKRETI

PENGUIN BOOKS

An imprint of Penguin Random House

PENGUIN BOOKS

USA | Canada | UK | Ireland | Australia
New Zealand | India | South Africa | China

Penguin Books is part of the Penguin Random House group of companies whose addresses can be found at global.penguinrandomhouse.com

Published by Penguin Random House India Pvt. Ltd
7th Floor, Infinity Tower C, DLF Cyber City,
Gurgaon 122 002, Haryana, India

Penguin Random House India

First published in Hindi as *Purnahuti* by National Publishing House, Jaipur 1990
Published in Penguin Books by Penguin Random House India 2017

Copyright © Mridula Behari 2017
English translation copyright © Mitranand Kukreti 2017

All rights reserved

10 9 8 7 6 5 4 3 2 1

This is a work of fiction. All situations, incidents, dialogue and characters, with the exception of some well-known historical and public figures mentioned in this novel, are products of the author's imagination and are not to be construed as real. They are not intended to depict actual events or people or to change the entirely fictional nature of the work. In all other respects, any resemblance to persons living or dead is entirely coincidental.

ISBN 9780143441335

Typeset in Adobe Garamond Pro by Manipal Digital Systems, Manipal
Printed at Thomson Press India Ltd, New Delhi

This book is sold subject to the condition that it shall not, by way of trade or otherwise, be lent, resold, hired out, or otherwise circulated without the publisher's prior consent in any form of binding or cover other than that in which it is published and without a similar condition including this condition being imposed on the subsequent purchaser.

www.penguin.co.in

To my mother, Annapurna Sinha

LEICESTER LIBRARIES	
Askews & Holts	18-Apr-2018
	£9.99

Preface

I do not remember how and when the idea of the story of Padmini, the Rajput queen of Chittor, took seed in my mind. But somewhere, the pebble of an idea dropped and the ripples it created stayed. Padmini was known for her surreal beauty. Literature has recorded how the extraordinary beauty of Helen of Troy and Cleopatra caused grief and misfortune. The story of Padmini, in medieval India, is yet another reiteration of this unpleasant truth. It stayed with me and I read everything I could about her in the ensuing years.

I have portrayed Padmini exactly as I saw her through my mind's eye. Was she merely a beautiful face? What were her thoughts, emotions and strengths? While writing this novel, I was careful with the descriptions of the surroundings, atmosphere, events and emotional nuances. This was to ensure that they conveyed the way this extraordinarily beautiful queen looked, thought, lived and suffered. But Padmini was not merely a beauty. She possessed an unbreakable tenacity of spirit and a sense of righteousness and responsibility in equal measure.

In order to collect material on the life and times of Padmini, I trawled through various libraries in Rajasthan. Each small and seemingly trivial detail that I picked up from the ocean of books gave me immense pleasure. While going through historical works, and later ruminating over them, I realized that while Indian society has changed in many ways, it is still the same in many others.

I wrote the beginning and end of this novel during my sojourn in Bikaner. During those days, my husband, Om Prakash Behari, a senior officer in the Indian Administrative Service, was posted there. Our residence was the grand Padma Nivas. I still wonder whether this story came to me as a mere coincidence or if my thought process was influenced by the ambience. When I started writing, I didn't know how far my destination was, but I did have a strong desire to proceed.

There was another important milestone associated with Padma Nivas. Before becoming the commissioner's residence, it housed the Rajasthan Oriental Research Institute. Muni Jinvijay, the late Padma Shri archaeologist and scholar, was its honorary director. Muni, who both worked and lived at Padma Nivas, was a great source of information on Padmini's life.

During all these years, I felt a sense of mystical support around me. Was the spirit of Padmini watching over me while I wrote? I would like to believe so. The characters of Sugna, a chief attendant, and Likhvanbai, another attendant, whom I have woven into this novel, have not been mentioned in any poetic work, book or folklore. I feel it was Padmini who conjured them up for me.

The legend of Padmini is well-known to the people of this country. Traditional bards and singers have been singing about her for years. The poets Malik Mohammad Jayasi and Hem Ratan, and the historians Farishta and Abul Fazal, have written about her glory. Jayasi, a contemporary of Sher Shah Suri (the other three lived later, during the time of Akbar), wrote the story of Padmini in poetic form for the first time. *Padmavat*, written in 1520 CE, included fictional incidents that lent romantic hues to the epic poem. Thus, some historians dismiss it as a figment of Jayasi's imagination. Others, however, give credence to the historicity of the events he described. Muni Jinvijay was one of them.

This novel is based on *Gora Badal Padmini Chaupai* by Hem Ratan, a little-known sixteenth-century work. Approximately seven decades ago, Muni Jinvijay chanced upon this work while surveying Jain archives. It took him a long time to collect and compile its different texts. It was due to the concerted efforts of Muni and his disciple Udai Singh Bhatnagar that it took on the form of a book in 1966.

There is some controversy regarding Padmini's place of birth. Hem Ratan described her as a princess of Singhal Dweep or present-day Sri Lanka. The well-known historian

Colonel Todd, the author of *Annals and Antiquities of Rajasthan*, was of the same opinion. But there appears to be no reason to believe that Padmini hailed from Sri Lanka. In many folktales, Poogal, a small town near Bikaner still known for the beauty of its women, has been described as her native place. The beautiful woman described in the famous folktale of love, 'Dhola Maru', belonged to Poogal. Padmini was the princess of the Pratihar dynasty that ruled Poogal during that time. However, these remain conjectures. It is for this reason that I have deliberately not mentioned Padmini's native place. In my heart, however, I believe she belongs to Poogal.

I have been fortunate to receive inputs from different people: a respected lady of Poogal provided an important piece of information; Suban Khan, who also belongs to the same place, gave me detailed information about the customs followed by royal families during marriage ceremonies; Sushilabai, wife of the former ruler of Bikaner, late Karni Singh, sourced significant information on this subject too. She herself is a direct descendant of the Sisod dynasty—the ruling family of Chittor. I also received valuable information about the rules, traditions and customs of royal families from a cross-section of people belonging to Rajput ruling dynasties. I am deeply grateful to all of them.

My novel ends with Rani Padmini performing *jauhar*, or self-immolation, to save her honour after Mewar was defeated at the hands of Ala-ud-Din Khilji in Vikram

Samvat (Vikram Era) 1360 (or 1303 CE). Chittor was then renamed Khizrabad. However, twenty-two years later, in Vikram Samvat 1382 (1325 CE), Hamir recaptured Mewar and Khizrabad became Chittor again. Under Hamir's rule, Chittor's power and honour reached new heights. A number of great warriors—Rana Kumbha, Rana Sanga and Maharana Pratap—were born into the Rajput dynasty.

The primary source of my information was the Rajasthan State Archives in Bikaner, which has a large number of books and documents on the state's history. Its former director Jitendra Kumar, a scholar of history, gave me useful material on Padmini. Kshama Sharma read out to me the poetry of Hem Ratan, written in Rajasthani, and took pains to explain it in detail. I am deeply indebted to all of them. Also, I am thankful to all the historians and writers whose works offered an insight into the world of Padmini.

Mridula Behari

Lost in thought, Padmini didn't realize when her *odhani* slipped off her head. Ratan Singh gazed at her longingly, at her voluptuous body elegantly dressed in diaphanous silks, her delicately-sculpted midriff . . . her lips retaining the innate winsome smile with no trace of trauma . . . the same liquid eyes of a doe, and her voice as sweet as the mellifluous notes emanating from the strings of a veena. The glow on her face, as bright as ever, radiated only love and yearning even as irresistible charm dripped from her eyes. Outside, a thousand moons showered their coolness as though attempting to quench the fire of passion. From far-off woods, beyond the royal garden, came the sound of joyous peacocks.

A cataclysmic terror gripped Mewar. A dense haze of fear and consternation had spread all over. Yet the pervasive shadow of gloom was not static. What was daunting was that the anxiety and fear only grew. Even the slightest footfall was enough to terrify people. The citizens of Mewar—which had survived countless wars—were unable to recollect a time when they had suffered such excruciating physical and mental trauma.

It was hard to believe that this was the same place that had, until a few days ago, been wrapped in a protective canopy of love and care. No trace of that contentment remained. Everything seemed obliterated by the ominous dark clouds gathering on the horizon. Ala-ud-Din Khilji, the ruler of Delhi, along with his mighty army, had reached Chittor. A grim sense of foreboding spread all around like a pall of smoke. An imminent sense of danger hung in the air. It seemed as if they were all on the brink; anything could happen at any time.

Chittor, the heart of Mewar, had weathered many storms. Senseless violence, brutality and large-scale destruction had swept the land; its skies had been on fire before. Yet, the centre of political and social activities had remained undaunted. How had Khilji's mere presence reduced the capital to a mere shadow of its past?

Since breaking into the palace-fort that housed a garrison of soldiers would have been next to impossible, Ala-ud-Din laid siege to the city of Chittorgarh. The movement of people was blockaded. Life came to a standstill. All activities, including business, came to a grinding halt.

The sultan's army plundered and killed, leaving behind a trail of devastation. Everything was in ruins. The wheel of oppression moved swiftly. Innocent men were slaughtered and women were raped. Bodies of villagers with their heads severed were presented to the sultan as war trophies. With each passing day, their atrocities grew more inhumane. Violence, bloodshed and arson—the horrors of death, destruction and ominous uncertainties loomed large.

There was no stopping the brazen show of brute force.

Sultan Khilji's royal edict, which was received some time ago, was like a dagger plunged into the back. It had shocked and horrified not only Maharawal Ratan Singh, the king of Mewar, but the rulers of all adjoining states, particularly those who refused to submit to the sultan and had chosen to maintain their sovereignty.

The royal edict, written on a scroll of silk, was a message from the sultan, a barbaric brute. It read: 'Rani Padmini, the beautiful queen of the royal dynasty of Mewar, shall be handed over to the sultan. Failing this, the sultan will wage a battle against the king of Mewar and take her away by force.'

In her room in the women's apartment of the palace, Padmini stood by the window. Her glowing skin and chiselled features radiated her youth. She was no ordinary beauty. Her hair, her slender figure and the perfection of each feature resembled that of a celestial damsel. But at that moment she looked like a cursed princess.

Padmini stared at the evening sun, its last shafts of light on the horizon. It seemed to portend the coming of a frightening, dark night. Her leaden eyes and shallow breathing seemed to reflect the failing light. A feeling of intense dejection had coiled up in her heart and seemed to have left her frozen.

Outside, the *badaran*s and *baandi*s, bondmaids of different ranks, were talking loudly. Sugna, the bridesmaid, was sitting on the floor and leaning against the wall, silently looking at her Ranisa. She watched as the setting winter sun seemed to paint the queen with golden translucence. She was troubled by the turbulence in the queen's mind. They had been close since they were children. Having lived in Padmini's company constantly, Sugna could read her mistress's mind from the expressions flitting on her visage.

She felt a knot of frustration building inside her when the queen, as if sensing Sugna's eyes on her, spoke without turning towards her. 'How horrid and devoid of any human feeling is the sultan to have invaded Chittor, Sugna! I've heard that today in Badnor he destroyed all the fields and the standing crops; dragged children out of their homes and killed them mercilessly; and dishonoured women. The devils spared no one.' Padmini's face was expressionless as the words poured out of her mouth, but Sugna knew that the queen's heart was filled with anguish.

Sugna hurried to assuage her anxiety. 'You need not worry. It is impossible for anybody to defeat our Kshatriyas, the brave warriors of this land. Even after causing so much death and destruction, he has not succeeded in his mission. Two months have passed since he besieged the fort; he is still far from his goal.'

'It is not so, Sugna!' Padmini's voice was low, as if lost in thought, as if talking to herself. 'This sultan is different from the other rulers of this great country, Aryavart. He doesn't follow any ethical principles in strategy-planning. He has violated each and every time-honoured principle of the battlefield. He has desecrated temples and idols of gods and goddesses.'

She paused, tucked an invisible strand of hair behind her ear, and continued, 'After sacking the kingdom of the Yadava king of Devagiri, Ramchandra, he took away his daughter Chhitai and married her, causing the king untold misery. And in Anahilpatan, during the period of the Baghela rulers, people lost their peace and happiness completely. His subedars, Ulug Khan and Alap Khan, ransacked the entire place and caused large-scale damage to life and property. Jain Acharya Kakkasuri narrated all this during his recent stay at the palace.'

'But how did he come to know? Wasn't he in Jabalipur at that time?' Sugna countered.

'He is the dharma guru of Samar Shah, the renowned trader of Anahilpatan, who is in close contact with Ulug Khan and Alap Khan. It is he who told Kakkasuri all that I have told you. He was telling us that they looted unique idols adorned with gold ornaments from the temple. The marauders walked off with the jewellery and melted the idols but not before damaging the noses. They broke into Jain temples and took away cartloads of precious statues, which they returned only after being paid a substantial amount. Not only this, Sugna! They brazenly abducted Malati Devi and Deval Kumari, the queens of the state, and presented them to the sultan of Delhi who kept them in his harem and treated them savagely. The sultan even wanted to take the queens and the daughter of Hamir, the king of Ranthambore, as prisoners and dump them in his hell-like harem. But before he could succeed, they jumped into the fire. He is an absolute monster. He considers only his sensual pleasure and nothing else. All his thoughts and deeds are centred around fulfilling his carnal desires. He makes fun of all ethical principles. He dismisses virtuousness as a mental aberration. None of the rulers, including Raja Karnadev, Raja Ramchandra and Raja Hamir, could escape his designs. He defeated all of them. The defeat of the rulers of his neighbouring states has weakened the maharawal's morale. The siege appears to be stretching endlessly. No propitious signs are in sight. The sultan has rampaged through village after village. Nobody knows when this trail of devastation will end.'

Sugna sighed in despair, adding, 'They say he is so arrogant and power-drunk that he doesn't listen to his own *qazi*s and mullahs. He is totally irreligious. Otherwise, why would he desecrate idols of Hindu deities? He treats his own wife as an enemy. He killed her father, Jalal-ud-Din, who was also his uncle, and usurped the throne.'

'What made him such a reckless butcher?' asked Padmini with a heavy heart. Taking a deep breath, she said, 'What could have made him so heartless? He thinks that it is his dharma to achieve everything that he wishes to. Why? Doesn't he realize that a warrior without compassion is only an oppressor indulging in indiscriminate bloodletting?'

Sugna stared back without answering.

After a moment's pause, Padmini continued, 'The Rana of Sisod, Bhad Lakshman Singh, is engaged in a fight with the enemies of Malwa. If he were here, he would have found a way out. There are others too, like Gora Rawat, but the maharawal is still annoyed with him.'

Sugna tried to calm her down saying, 'Why are you so worried, Raj Rani? This will prove to be as transient as the passing clouds. Moreover, the maharawal is here to protect us all. There is no reason for you to be so worried.'

'No, it isn't so, Sugna! He has changed. He is always confused. He doesn't seem to be able to think clearly or take a decision. Always consumed by guilt, he thinks he is responsible for this sorry state of affairs. Where have his heroic brilliance, his innate energy and agility, and his witty Kshatriya nature gone?'

'Why don't you reason with him that it is all due to the vicissitudes of the destiny of a ruler, that the astrologers of the state and the Raj Purohits Pallival are doing everything they can to placate the malevolent stars.'

'He does not listen. All he says is that we were busy in merrymaking and had lost touch with our fighting skills. Our enemy is an expert in guerrilla warfare. Our soldiers may be brave, but is that enough? They are not equipped with present-day weapons and techniques. We didn't do anything to upgrade our arsenal. And he would never consider the easy way out: that of disgracefully laying down his arms before the enemy. He would revolt against the very idea.' Padmini found her voice cold and spiritless.

'Even Lord Shiva performs *lasya,* the amorous dance form, but that does not mean he'll shy away from performing the *tandava,* the dance of annihilation,' said Sugna. 'You should have convinced him forcefully that debilitating self-condemnation, self-pity and helplessness have no place in a king's life.' After a moment's pause, looking at her queen, she added quietly, 'You should never forget that even though the doer is a man, it is always a woman who inspires him to take up challenges. It is the inspiring words of a woman that set a man on the right path. There's no doubt that your emotional support will motivate him to face this critical situation with renewed valour and zeal.'

'But how am I to do it? He comes, stays for a while, and leaves. Strung-up, weary, ill-at-ease, he's always lost in thought, struggling with heaven-knows-what problems,' said the queen. 'Day and night, he is haunted by conflicts and nightmares. Sometimes, I think he can't see things clearly. It seems as if he is fighting continuously; with his enemies, with himself. At times, I feel that he has lost confidence in himself, in his own potential.' Trying to blink back tears, Padmini continued, 'Two months have passed since a camp was set up between Gambhiri and Berach. How long will this spate of killings, this senseless violence continue? When will this mindless bloodshed stop?'

'Don't trouble yourself needlessly. Believe me, these alien invaders will never be able to intrude into this sacred fort,' said Sugna, trying to console her queen. But before she could add anything, Padmini said, 'A peace treaty has been sent today. A meeting of the council of ministers is also scheduled. Let's see what decision they take. My heart is beating very fast. I don't know why, but it feels like something disastrous is in the offing. There's no knowing what that devil is up to . . .'

'Please don't lose heart. Outside your chamber, a group of songsters is waiting to entertain you. They want to sing *patmanjari* classical music. If you want some other form of melody, they can sing Gunkali, which is set on the notes of raga Malkauns. The soothing notes will calm you down.'

'No, not now. I want to be by myself, absolutely undisturbed. Close the doors. The attendants outside are engaged in conversation and that disturbs me.'

* * *

After Sugna left, a strange dullness clogged her mind. Padmini stared out of the oriel as though she had lost her bearings. Atop a hillock in Chitravali, she could see the white tent of the sultan. The evening sky looked deserted. A dark, frightening lull before the storm seemed to be spreading all around.

If the king looked out of his window, what would he see? Would he also see the white tips of the sultan's tents? And if he did, what would his thoughts be? Padmini sometimes saw herself standing next to him and looking outside with him. And sometimes, she tried to slip into his mind. It tortured her to worry about him, to think for him and to watch him without being able to do anything.

A strange incapacity seemed to have taken over the king. He looked agitated and exhausted all the time. Had he decided to leave everything to destiny? If one tried to ask him anything, he did not respond. Instead, he would let out a deep sigh and look out of the window, fixing his gaze at some distant object. If he did open his mouth to speak, more often than not, he would stop mid-sentence and complete the unsaid part with facial expressions and gestures. It was pointless asking him to complete what he had intended to say.

Since the fort had come under siege, he had lost his appetite and sleep. His tense visage, a deep furrow appearing every now and then between his brows and his bloodshot eyes were all signs of his fast deteriorating condition. Self-condemnation and remorse had taken their toll. His face had lost much of its glow. The queen helplessly watched her husband, the king, growing more and more despondent, demoralized and weary.

In the few years that they had been together, he had become so attached to her that the very idea of surrendering and being separated from her was driving him mad. Or was it?

Sometimes Rani Padmini wondered if she, too, would go mad. Quite often, a devilish figure appeared in her dreams and chased her. Sometimes, she imagined that a monster-like animal had pounced on her. She would struggle frantically to free herself from its vice-like grip, kicking and punching, scratching its face, pulling its hair, and digging her fingernails and teeth into its arm. Yet its grip would not slacken, its muscular arms were extraordinarily strong. At times, she visualized an ugly ghost standing before her, staring at her, and then finding her terrified, letting out a roar of laughter.

She was not left undisturbed even if she did fall asleep exhausted. She dreamt of venomous snakes winding themselves around her body, and various species of horrible-looking wild animals with sharp claws advancing towards her. She would wake up with a jolt. Even after realizing it was a dream, she would be unable to stop shivering for a long time.

Her heart often sank without reason. She caught her reflection sometimes to see her eyes looking petrified. When she spoke, she had to reign in the quiver in her voice. She feared her body would fall lifeless if she didn't hold herself up.

Should she go to Prabhavati, the principal consort of the king, and talk to her? It was impossible to live with this burden on her mind, she told herself. She wanted to share with the older queen the ominous uncertainties clogging her mind. Perhaps, if she went and spoke to Prabhavati, the unburdening would deliver some peace of mind. Somewhere within her, she believed that even if vastly apart, they could help each other and salve their individual consciences to some extent.

But why has she chosen to keep me at an arm's length even now, when so much has happened? She should have forgotten the grudge she has been nursing against me. Why has she not reached out and shown me the courtesy of asking how I feel during this critical hour?

If this is her attitude, should I even go to her? Would she show any affinity? Who knows, I may find her all the more cold and distant. There is no knowing what prickly comment she may come up with, which may further embitter whatever has been left between us in the name of a relationship. She is the master of hurtful comments. Why should I expect any sympathetic response? One cannot expect any love and affection from her. It is impossible for her to say any kind words to me.

Padmini couldn't forget that it was because of her Prabhavati had been deprived of all that was due to her. She suddenly felt contrite. This was the reason why she was so ill-disposed towards her, wasn't it? What did she want, Padmini thought. All along, she had been trying to offer selfless love and trust and expected the same. But the *patrani* would not give her an opportunity to say anything . . .

Padmini wanted to sit and cry. She wanted to be held and rocked.

Memories of Mother are ever so sweet. The neem tree at my mother's place must be in full bloom now . . . the warm breeze filled with its pleasant smell would be blowing gently . . . the tiny, short-lived flowers on the ground would be peeping up. Somewhere on the endless expanse of sand, under the sparse shade of the khejri, *some mother will be telling her daughter the story of the two sisters: Taru and Maru. I, too, liked to listen to stories. It is through stories that I learned mathematics, art, logic, literature, scriptures and music.*

Once, an eminent astrologer had visited Tamragarh. He was an erudite and righteous Brahmin known for his scholarship. Mother had invited the acharya to her chambers. On his arrival, she had asked him to carefully study the stars of the daughter of the Pratihar Pawar king and foretell her future.

At her mother's insistence, little Padma had come forward, taken a seat close to the acharya, and extended her palms before him. The acharya had narrowed his eyes and fixed his gaze on the lines criss-crossing her hand. After quite some time, he raised his head and said, 'The lines on her hands clearly predict that she will earn a lot of fame, honour and glory. I can see that a great religious ritual will be performed by her. She will be the wife of a great king and accompany him at a *mahayajna,* a great sacrificial ritual like *vajpeya, rajsuya* or *ashwamedha.*'

Flushed with pride, little Padma had watched her mother beam as though her heart had turned into a heaven-kissing tower of joy and a vast ocean of love at the same time . . .

That heaven-kissing tower, alas, has collapsed like a house of cards and my breathtaking beauty has become a curse. The fame and glory of the exquisiteness of your daughter's beauty and grace has spread like a creeper of venom. O Mother! Everything is finished except this unending heart-wrenching pain. Your Padma has been put at stake.

O Eklinga! You are the protector of Mewar and know everything, omniscient as you are. Why don't you listen to the cries of my heart?

Smoke arose from somewhere. On its way to an unknown destination, it further darkened the already grey sky. A depressing gloom was perched on the turrets and battlements of the fort.

Is it the same Mewar? How different it looks from what it was. There is nothing to suggest that I ever lived here. Everything appears so hazy beyond that dense fog.

She continued to gaze into space . . . just looking, not seeing. But in that 'not seeing', reeling in her mind was her first sight of this land. It seemed like decades, yet it was only a few years ago. She was transported to the time when she first came here: the exhilarating breeze, the mild rosy fragrance in the air, and the thrill of a young bride looking at the opulence and prosperity that seemed to stretch as far as the eye could see.

An elaborately decorated chariot was rushing towards Chittor. It was followed by a dozen others, all running synchronously. Seated inside the royal chariot were Maharawal Ratan Singh of Mewar and his new bride, Rani Padmini. The accompanying chariots carried the bride's trousseau boxes containing precious jewellery, sets of dresses and bridal ensemble, gold and silverware, and several other gifts. A cavalcade of the soldiers of Mewar provided security cover.

A cool breeze stirred the trees. A sweet fragrance wafted along. The king gently pushed aside the silk curtains of the royal chariot. The golden and silver veil of the bride fluttered in the breeze. His imagination began to take wing.

Outside, a vast and unknown landscape swung into view. Clusters of sprawling bushes, shrubs, creepers, twined vines and plants raced past, leaving behind innumerable mounds and hills, step-wells, roundabouts and forest land.

They had almost reached Mewar.

As if sensing this, the horses ran faster, pulling the chariots with great speed. The curtains flew upward, tearing into the blue screen of the sky. Padmini, the bride, looked out of the partly covered window and watched the distant view with wonder, her eyes widening in astonishment at every new thing she encountered.

This is quite a new world; so different from the city governed by my father. There, a little drizzle here and there during the rainy season, and after that the land was dry all over. It was a vast expanse of desert and nothing else.

After crossing a distance of stony soil, they moved towards a beautiful verdant land, dark green shrubbery, thick forests and an ever-expanding blue sky. It was exquisite. The silence of the river that glittered in the sun was broken by the giggling water around the rocks. The mountain range, with its hilltops and peaks standing erect as if raising their proud heads, delighted her. The wind was unabated like the stream. Padmini looked in wonder at a flock of birds in the sky. What was it in the core of this land that pulled everything, every single particle, towards it? The tranquillity of the environment seemed to touch her instantly, creating a feeling of fondness, as if she had been connected to the place from another lifetime.

The chariot continued to race towards Chittor.

The lush surroundings looked so beautiful. Women, dressed in traditional red and yellow lehngas, worked in the fields. And over there, sitting in the shade of a tree,

Padmini saw a young woman nursing an infant while gazing at it lovingly.

Quite an eyeful, the alluring sights of this exquisite dreamland set her heart soaring.

The chariot jolted along the bumpy track. With every jerk, some part of her body would brush against the maharawal's well-built, sculpted physique. He seemed to be giving off an aura of aristocratic and majestic elegance. It sent a wave of thrill down her spine. The flush of excitement and her natural shyness made her withdraw. A tender, warm feeling of elation overtook her. Ripples of sweetness spread through her.

The world is so beautiful! She felt sure of this for the first time.

Padmini would have given everything to steal a glance at the king. But her innate modesty did not allow her to meet his gaze. Every now and then, she looked at his pagri, his headgear lying next to her. The *kilangi*, the crest of the pagri, had been encrusted with precious gems. Mother got it designed with all her fondness. Close to the pagri were golden *suparis*, betel leaves and coconut.

The city of Chittor swept into view, pulling her eyes towards it once again. At the edge of the hilly region stood the vast plains where, atop a large mount, stood the fort in all its glory.

The closer they reached, the faster the chariot seemed to go. On the way, the king hadn't said much. Along with the racing chariot, all kinds of thoughts galloped through Padmini's mind.

Is he taciturn by nature or are some matters of the state engaging his mind? What kind of person will the king turn out to be? Is he calm, serious, arrogant or emotional? How will he behave with me? From his deep, mild voice he seems sweet-natured. Is his tone nice only because he is talking to a bride? Will he change after a few days of living together? His hands will be full with the affairs of the state, his responsibilities relating to the protection of the interests of the state, meetings with artists and art connoisseurs. Will he have time for poor Padma?

Also, the queen consort will be there. Will she welcome me? What will be my response to her questions?

With the destination approaching, Padmini's heart raced.

The speed of the chariot dropped.

After covering some distance, it came on to Raj Marg, a boulevard leading to the palace. Thus, the chariot completed the long and tedious journey, arriving at the place it had set out for.

The arched gateways of the city were decked with flowers. Each and every door, window and screened balcony had been intricately decorated, as if every citizen of Mewar was clamouring for a glimpse of the queen of beauty: Rani Padmini. *Akshat,* coloured grains of rice, kumkum, saffron, flowers and garlands were showered on the chariot. The city resounded with drum rolls and the sound of rapturous music coming from traditional instruments. The joy and euphoria of the people had reached a fever pitch.

* * *

Rani Padmini stepped into the magnificent palace decorated with festoons of flowers and golden urns filled with water.

Attendants stood at the entrance with their hands folded down to their elbows. They bent low to greet her.

The ceremonial worship of the family deity was performed.

The sun began to dip behind a screen of dark green foliage.

That night, a grand celebration was organized to welcome the newly-wed Padmini. Every house was decorated with rows of lights. Every elegant building shone and glittered as if the city had decided to compete with the starlit skies.

There were joyous celebrations. The palace was bustling with chirpy and smiling attendants and female artistes including singers, musicians, drummers and bondmaids. It was a royal mela. The atmosphere was ecstatic with a riot of colours. Women dressed in multi-coloured sequined ghaghra-odhanis sashayed in and out, their jewellery tinkling and their voices lilted. They broke into giggles and raucous laughter. The merriment was infectious and even old crones caught the fervour, adding to the atmosphere with the irrepressible childlike curiosity of catching a glimpse of the bride, their new rani.

The moment Padmini raised her *ghunghat*, it seemed as if the moon had appeared in the queen's chamber. Her beauty would, in fact, put the moon of *purnima* to shame. There were already murmurs about her beauty, of the poetry that spun out of the lips of those who had seen her. So, there were those eager to see her and those who waited to scoff at the beauty they had only heard about. Yet, when the ghunghat was gently raised, it rendered everyone speechless.

The new queen looked as fragile and fragrant as a newly-bloomed *ketaki* flower. Everyone who caught a glimpse knew that every word they had heard about her, every single word, was true.

She was breathtaking. Was it the last lights of the setting sun or was she really aglow? Her skin had the golden lustre of the *champa* flower. With a round face, big luminescent eyes, delicate ruddy cheeks, thin, leaf-shaped lips, she seemed like the moon, no, the full moon light that streamed down during *sharad ritu*, the autumn. Her radiance dispelled the dark clouds of despondency. With lush black hair bedecked with flowers, arms like the stalks of lotus and feet painted red with henna, the lovely Padmini seemed ethereal. Her beauty was comparable only to that of an imagined *devakanya*, a celestial maiden. In fact, they were certain that celestial damsels like Rambha, Revati and Menaka would pale in comparison.

She looked as pure as the Ganga and seemed as charming as the *brahma kamal*.

When they could finally say something, when the spell she cast with her loveliness was broken, it was to utter just one word: 'Wah!'

Never in the court of Mewar or outside had anyone experienced the spell of an out-of-the-world beauty. The buzz grew. In the main courtyard of Padmini Mahal, the aroma from incense sticks rendered the mandap pleasantly fragrant. Young women flitted about with their anklets jingling, carrying fans made with peacock feathers, *chanwar*—a whisk made with the tails of yak—and other ornamentations. These young women and their attendants had all been engaged in the service of Padmini, who was now seated in the middle of the pavilion. Standing in one corner was a group of professional dancers in glittering dresses and ornaments.

The new queen was overwhelmed with the love and affection showered on her. From beneath her veil she looked shyly at the festivities.

It looked as though the night, intoxicated with beauty and glamour, would last for eternity. Noticing the spellbound dancers, their old lady-caretaker addressed them derogatorily, 'O dancing girls, will you present your performance or keep looking at Ranisa with your eyes wide open?'

'Why not, *kaki?* I will dance all night. Do you think any of us will be able to sleep a wink?' asked one lotus-eyed dancer excitedly, fluttering her eyelashes in a suggestive manner.

The attendants chortled in delight.

'Then go ahead.'

'Kaki, let Dhara Deviji sing the welcome song first,' said an attendant endearingly.

Dhara Devi, the renowned singer of Mewar, rose from her seat and came forward. She bowed to the gathering reverentially.

She closed her beautiful black eyes meditatively. Then her voice rose huskily. It was her own composition and she rendered it, note for sweet note, in her seductive voice, taking pleasure in the various tenors and the emotion of the ragini. Her singing was accompanied by the soft notes of the sarangi. The delicate waves created by the sound from the veena held her mellifluous voice. Gradually, she moved on from the palpable to impalpable, from material to spiritual. As if in a trance, the audience swayed in unmitigated bliss.

The night was unprecedented in all its glory. It was difficult to say whether darkness was encroaching on the light or the other way round. After Dhara Devi's virtuoso performance, dancers wearing *nupur* on their ankles took over the stage. The tiny bells attached to their anklets began to jingle with the swift footwork of the dancers, in tandem with the varying rhythms of the mridangam and other percussion instruments. All the dancers were adept in the nuances of deft eye movements, lifts of the eyebrows, suggestive side glances and quick footwork, which made them spiral into a blur. In the backdrop, singers crooned: 'I wish my *chunar* was dyed in the colour of your turban, dear husband. Let our bodies meet the way our hearts have met.'

The dancers, overwhelmed by the love and ecstasy that the music evoked, conveyed the emotions through different parts of their bodies: postures, hand formations, and footwork. Their jewelled bracelets sparkled and rang with every movement. Dancing to the swift rhythmic patterns, they looked like colourful bouquets swaying in the air. The agility, the litheness of the dancers and the wonderful recital left Padmini astonished.

The performance and badinage continued late into the night. The performers were rewarded lavishly in consideration of their status.

Then, unexpectedly, a special message was received. The chief queen, Maharani Prabhavati from Prabha Mahal, had sent word that she wanted to see Padmini before the second phase of the night was over. Her word was an order in the women's apartment of the palace. As per palace protocol, the position of the maharani was high. In view of this, it was obligatory for Padmini to go and meet her immediately. Meeting the maharani was integral in Padmini's mind too, and she would have asked for a meeting herself had she been allowed to speak. Well versed in palace decorum, Padmini had been eager to see Maharani Prabhavati right from the start.

Without further ado, she rose. A group led her to the older queen's palace. Padmini walked down the corridor at a leisurely pace, examining every crevice with irrepressible curiosity. Following her were Sugna, Magan, Chhagan, Chand and some other attendants. The moon of the *shukla paksha* was high in the sky. The moonlight bathed everything in a soft luminescence.

And then, they were there.

As Padmini entered the residential wing of Prabha Mahal, her entourage from her parental home was awestruck by the magnificence of the structure, while those from Rani Prabhavati's palace were amazed by the new queen.

As soon as Padmini arrived at the doorway of the maharani's room, the bondmaids raised the heavy blue curtains on both sides. It was awash with soft, soothing light and filled with the aroma of burning incense, the magical spell of the aristocratic ambience, and layers and layers of mystery. With Padmini walking in, a ray of light seemed to have entered a space that was as quiet as an autumn cloud.

And then she saw her. And how did she not see her before this? Something flowing inside Padmini stopped all of a sudden.

Backed by self-confidence and experience, Rani Prabhavati was sitting on a raised, ornately carved chair in a domineering manner, as though she had tamed all the hubris of the potentates of the world. Her jewellery, studded with rubies, sapphires, diamonds and other gems, along with her brocade attire, was a dazzling, brazen display of ostentation and hauteur. Padmini was awestruck. She is the maharani, she told herself; she was in the presence of Raj Rani Prabhavati, the queen consort and mother of the future king of the Guhil dynasty.

Padmini took time to look at the woman examining her. That she was used to a life of luxury was apparent from every gesture. Her countenance reflected intellect and character. Proud of her beauty, she rested her elbow nonchalantly on a soft silken bolster, as though Padmini was not too much of a presence to take cognizance of. It was as if she was the sole empress of this empire. She was flanked by two attendants gently waving huge fans made of peacock feathers. Neither looked at or acknowledged anybody but the queen they were bound to. Padmini bowed her forehead in reverence and greeted her by joining her delicate hands. The maharani seemed to look through her without as much as a faint smile. With a slight movement of her eyebrows, she signalled to her attendants for Padmini to sit. Padmini sat on a comparatively smaller chair with trepidation. With a frown of pride on her brow, she gave Padmini a reproachful glance. That she was displeased was only too obvious from her expression.

Tension hung in the air like the stretched string of a bow. Padmini found her heart racing. She raised her eyes once again, but her timid glance was not met with a kind expression. They were looking at some point above or beside her and her entourage. Padmini suddenly felt as if strong vines bound her head to toe. She felt herself shrink in such an unfriendly presence. If only Padmini knew the effect she had on the maharani and her ladies-in-waiting. It took a huge amount of effort from the maharani's court to not succumb to her beauty and charming personality. The maharani, who was struck by Padmini's beauty, tried to find a flaw. Nothing. She felt a stab of pain, and her face froze in dismay. Only the maharani's overweening consciousness of her position kept her emotions reined in. She behaved as though there was nothing extraordinary in Padmini's appearance. Fighting the warmth radiating from the young queen, the maharani stared at her, as though trying to read something written on her face.

Feeling inferior, Padmini realized that the maharani reigned supreme in the women's apartment and that she was adept in the art of making the other person feel small without saying a word. Her face fell. The maharani noted this with pleasure.

An overbearing Maharani Prabhavati said, 'Our lives will, henceforth, run parallel. So you would do well to know, and be within, your limits.' Her tone was cold and distant.

Her words cut Padmini to the quick. A spark of anger flickered, but she hastily quelled it. Her ears turned red. How was she to react to this order? She chose to keep quiet even as an eloquent silence hung in the room.

The maharani turned her heavily bejewelled neck slightly and said, 'Do you understand?'

Padmini, subdued as she was, simply nodded. It wouldn't do to show how hurt she was. She lowered her head and blinked back tears.

The air became heavy. Padmini felt very uncomfortable. Suddenly every second seemed imperceptibly long. The more she tried to stay normal, the more uncomfortable she felt.

If that was not enough, Prabhavati looked at Padmini with fierceness in her eyes and added, 'I know the nature of the raja. Do not ever try to cast your spell on him.' Her words had a distinct ring of arrogance.

With this, she turned her head away. The precious gem on her nose stud emitted a piercing sparkle as if cautioning Padmini.

Padmini held herself stiffly, her eyes still on the carpet, deeply hurt.

'Sona!' commanded the maharani.

An attendant came forward with her head bowed and hands folded.

'Has Manimala come?'

'Yes, Your Highness!'

'Send her in immediately. I want her to sing *Tank Magha Raga* to me in complete solitude.'

The words rang out loud, a clear indication that Padmini had been dismissed.

Such harshness. Such lack of grace. *What did you expect*, Padmini chided herself. The joy she felt at being a bride was shattered. One unbending person had cast a shadow so dark that all the sparkle in the world would be unable to pierce it. She was in a place where carrying out the maharani's order was the sole diktat. She stood rooted for a few awkward moments and then quietly turned around and left.

She felt free. In one stroke, the maharani had freed her from working on the bonds of love and a relationship.

Behind her, the silk curtain came down rustling.

Just as she was exiting, her eyes fell on a young boy of about fifteen or sixteen years of age. His face had the glow of a flame. Chand, one of the attendants, introduced him to her, 'He is Patvi Kanwar Veerbhan, the son of the maharani.'

Veerbhan, the crown prince and future king of Mewar.

Padmini returned to her room. It was only when she reached the confines of her room that she realized that she had been holding her breath all this while. She exhaled shakily and drew in a deep breath. The air was fragrant here and seemed lighter. The air *there* felt as if it were made of lead. She shut her eyes and opened them, blinking rapidly. The eyes of Maharani Prabhavati, it seemed, were still chasing her. How penetrating they were, capable of seeing through others' secret thoughts and, at the same time, vigilant enough to not allow anyone to read hers! And the tone of her voice? How clipped and cutting it was, capable of striking at the most vulnerable emotions of the other person. It was still ringing in her ears. At the very outset, she had made it abundantly clear that she was displeased with this new relationship.

Padmini felt as if a splinter had lodged itself in her flesh and was piercing deeper and deeper. It left her with a heavy heart.

When Sugna was the only attendant left in the room, Padmini exclaimed, 'Sugna, how rude and unceremonious she was!'

'Yes, as if someone with injured pride was hissing furiously. But why blame her? She, too, is a woman, and for a woman it is the greatest pain to see her husband married again,' said Sugna, trying to soothe her mistress's ruffled emotions.

'How triumphant was her demeanour!'

'But didn't you notice her eyes? Deep down, there were signs of unmitigated agony. That's why she wanted to listen to the *Tank Magha Raga*. Only one whose heart is torn with the pangs of separation would want this raga sung at midnight.'

'I was completely mystified. All I could understand was that she was trying to cover something that was going on inside her.'

'The ego is quite insuppressible, Ranisa! It does not allow you to admit defeat even when you are totally routed.'

'How painful it must have been for her to know that her husband had married another woman, leaving her out in the cold.'

'It is this disarming plain-heartedness that further stirred her envy . . . she was *not* left out in the cold as you say, Ranisa. When the song and dance programme was on, Magan, who was sitting behind me, told me that the maharawal had made certain commitments to her. He has promised her that he will accept all her terms and that she will continue to enjoy the highest position in the palace protocol. The sedan chair, in which she will be seated, will lead others in any procession. On all festivals, he will spend the night with the maharani. Also, as a gesture of honour, title-deeds of a number of villages have been designated in her name. The expenses incurred on various services and amenities provided to her, from the maintenance of storehouses to her midwives, are commensurate with her status and privilege. Even in seemingly small matters, like the provision of the paired paans, her share of betel leaves is larger than that of anybody else.'

Sugna was secretly jubilant at having collected so much information in such a short time. Just as she was gloating over her scouting prowess, she noticed that her mistress was unresponsive. Deflated, she realized that in her self-congratulatory mood, she had missed the fact that she was unwittingly causing more hurt to her mistress. She hastily added, 'But the fact remains that your arrival is her defeat in every way. This kind of behaviour on her part is telling of her discomfiture.'

'She knows well how to bear the pain of defeat. But, Sugna, I can't understand why the maharawal decided to remarry when he already had such a beautiful wife.'

Sugna smiled at her innocence and said, 'Do you remember what Gujar Dhai, that midwife, had said? "A man's mind is not so disciplined that he would never be attracted to another woman either before or after his marriage. A man has his own way of loving a woman. A man's love has a force of passion, but it lacks constancy and depth. This is why a woman has to use physical charm and winsome ways to keep her husband under control. These mysterious ways of a woman are both her ornament and her armament. The formation of this creation, the *srishti*, is rooted in the woman and her wiles."'

Padmini intoned, 'A woman is not made only to allure, delight or inspire a man. She has her own place in life which is, in effect, a yajna, a sacrificial rite.'

Sugna tried to divert her thoughts and said, 'This is no time to waste our breath on such things. You've got to dress up afresh. I'll help you with your make-up. This is your first night in the palace.'

Padmini shook herself from her stupor. One cold reception had made her forget that. She gave Sugna a mischievous smile and said, 'You too go to your room and adorn yourself with cosmetics, jewellery and fine dresses for your first night. Maldeva must be waiting for you restlessly.'

After Sugna left, Padmini reverted to her stream of thoughts. She was transported back to the queen's room, once again getting a dressing down . . . She smarted from the sense of inferiority that had gripped her when she had faced the maharani. Something gnawed at her insides.

It is not easy for the maharani to put up with what has happened. It is quite natural for her to hold a grudge against me and to lash out. But then, how am I to blame? What is my fault? I have handed my whole life over to her without any malice. She should accept the situation. We should make efforts to maintain trust and understanding.

Unable to delve into Prabhavati's mind, she felt a whirlpool swirling inside her.

But the amorous silence that prevailed in the royal bedchamber drew her out. Aromatic oil lamps reminded her of the night to come. Hanging from the high ceilings and engraved with delicate patterns, chandeliers with gem-studded lamps swung gently in the breeze. Strings of sapphires and pearls that hung on the doors and windows swayed too, their tiny holders emitting soothing sounds. On either side of the room, close to the oriel, the nuptial bed was studded with rubies.

Padmini was bathed, scented and adorned with *solah shringar,* the sixteen steps of beautification. From head to toe, she was bedecked opulently in dazzling pieces of jewellery: bracelets, armlets, necklace, dangling earrings, nose ring and *maang tika*. She was dressed in a silver brocade ghaghra with intricate crimson floral motifs and a sequined blouse. A sheer yellow lace odhani covered her head. She was made to sit in the centre of the nuptial bed that was draped with a velvet sheet strewn with ochre and yellow petals of the *patal* flower.

That is when Padmini realized that the music had stopped. It almost seemed as if the palace, like the bride, waited in hushed anticipation. A light fragrance wafted into the room.

The attendants had left, all of them turning to take a last look at the goddess who sat waiting demurely. Padmini trembled slightly as she bowed her head and waited, holding her breath. The slightest movements made her jewellery tinkle.

Then she heard him. He had walked in. From within her ghunghat that partially veiled her face, and through lowered eyelashes, Padmini surreptitiously tried to catch a glimpse of Ratan Singh. She noted his large forehead, his long sharp nose, his slightly upturned chin, his determined lips, his broad shoulders and height. Her breath was caught in her throat. He was very handsome indeed.

Ratan Singh walked towards her. And then he was in front of her, lifting her ghunghat slowly. Suddenly, he stopped as if struck. What he saw left him spellbound. Glowing in divine beauty, his new queen sat still, holding her breath, her eyes closed. The king was unable to move or to look elsewhere as he gazed unwaveringly at the exquisite beauty before him. It was as if he was facing Rati, a celestial beauty and the wife of Kamdeva, the god of love, in his dream.

Slowly, as if in a trance, he placed a finger under her chin and lifted her head. No longer able to keep her eyes closed, Padmini tremulously lifted her gaze. She saw love springing from the king's eyes, unnamable bliss on his face. Her husband was infatuated. Padmini, too, was almost unable to control her emotions. An internal strength of restraint just about kept her tethered. Her eyes shone with elation. Overwhelmed with emotions, she lowered her eyes again.

Speechless, enchanted and overwhelmed, Ratan Singh found himself bound by an ineffable attraction. Choked with emotion, he said dreamily, 'How do I take my eyes off your beautiful face! They have turned into parched pits with unquenchable thirst.'

She was surprised by the tone of his voice, which was soft, calm and musical. There was no trace of the dignified seriousness he had used to address others en route to Chittor.

He reached out for a goblet of wine, sipping the drink and taking in the intoxicating beauty of his new wife. Floating in an ocean of grace and charm, unable to come ashore, he tucked aside a ringlet of her hair. He then kissed her long thick eyelashes. She blushed. The colour that rose on her cheeks made her all the more attractive.

There was untrammelled joy in the air.

He took her into his arms lovingly and held her close against his broad chest, as though he wanted to inhale her musky fragrance in one breath. Pleasure rustled like silk. His scent permeated her body. He made love to her tenderly. How could anyone sleep on a magical night like this?

Thrilled by the touch of a hitherto unknown pleasure, Padmini woke up to the enchanting light of the first rays of dawn. Still in bed, she could see the blurry sunrise through a colourful glass window.

For an instant, she wondered where she was. Then the events of the momentous evening gone by came back to her. The palace! She was married! Innocent curiosity made her walk towards the window. Last night, she had seen the palace lit with diyas. Now she wanted to see it bathed in sunlight. She pushed the window open, inhaled the dewy morning air and watched dawn break. First, one part of the distant hills was kissed by its light, then the next, then another.

The entire mountain range is gleaming with a golden halo . . . The dark green cloud-shaped trees are shining in the soft sunlight. In the clear blue sky, a few balls of light clouds are floating over green fields. In the valley, the spire of a temple peeps out from behind thickets of trees and bushes.

A squeaky clean white temple, dark and deep woods, wide fertile fields, all bask in the saffron sunlight. The earth looks fresh, as though it had been bathed in molten gold.

She was overtaken by a sense of awe for the beauty her eyes were feasting on.

She continued to gaze at the mountain range, submerged in the shadowy world between dream and wakefulness.

'Padma! That is the Aravali range. Do you know what the word "Aravali" means?'

She turned towards her husband, who lay on the bed with his elbow resting on a round bolster. A sense of contentment was visible on his face. Dressed in scented silk, he looked relaxed.

She felt a surge of happiness and smiled at him softly. In response, a gracious smile flashed on the king's lips, lighting up his face. Suddenly nothing was important. Only him. The memory of the previous night made her blush. With her spirits soaring, she stood there, uncertain if she should walk back to him or stay there at the window with an open view to the world outside and her world inside.

They gazed at each other, unable to speak. Then, full of emotion, he said, 'You are special to me. Believe me, I feel as if I have known you for forever.'

The room was now suffused with bright sunlight. Delighted, she said shyly, 'Aravali.'

'Yes,' he laughed. 'Aravali means rugged and craggy landscape.'

So drawn was she to him that she didn't realize she had walked back, still gazing at him. Ratan Singh, too, unable to take his eyes off her for even a minute, said, 'You have made nature as a whole, its flora and fauna, so very attractive. They, along with you, have assumed a new look.'

There was a curiosity in Padmini's eyes, which Ratan Singh had no difficulty reading.

Not knowing what else to say, he continued, 'During the Mahabharat era, Bhim, the son of Pandu, got this fort constructed. Many, many years later, the Maurya king Chitrak renovated it and gave it its new name, Chitrakoot. Now, it is known as Chittor. In the ancient texts, it has been called Madhyamika.'

Padmini listened to him attentively.

'With the passage of time, our ancestor from the Guhil dynasty, Bapa Rawal, established his kingdom there. A siddha sage named Harit Muni blessed him and said that he would lay the foundations of the biggest empire in Aryavart. Inspired by Harit Muni, Bapa Rawal became a devotee and worshipper of Lord Eklingji. Even today, Lord Eklingji is our family deity. Bapa was a brave warrior. He had defeated invaders coming from the Sindh side. That's why he is called "the Sun of the Hindus". Even today, Chittor is a unique land of the brave.'

Padmini soaked in all the information and looked at him eagerly, wishing to hear more.

'You can call Likhvanbai to your room and seek more information. She knows a lot about this royal family and its history,' responded the king, reading her expression correctly.

He placed his hand on his bride's shoulder and raised himself. Then, changing into his long royal robes, he left the room.

After he left, Padmini moved languidly and looked at the paintings on the wall. She stopped in front of one, considering it unblinkingly.

The painting was that of an extremely beautiful woman as comely as Rati, fair with large eyes, dressed in a red corset, a white odhani over her head, and a golden ghaghra covering her waist downward. At the centre was a golden temple of Lord Shiva with a white *shivalinga* inside. Facing the sanctum sanctorum, the woman—the *nayika* or heroine—was seated on a giant lotus flower paying obeisance to Lord Shiva by clapping her hands.

Just like the music Padmini had been privy to, the painting drew her into mystic sensuousness. Padmini was lost in wandering thoughts and wayward emotions . . .

* * *

All notes of the melodious music lay dead on the quivering strings of the sarangi. The visage of the king, etched in her heart and mind, stayed intact. But the mirthful nights, still intoxicated by the opulent past, were lost in the desert of stark reality like footprints on shifting sand.

The trees and flowers swaying in the breeze, the sweet smell of freshly wet earth, those days of seemingly everlasting togetherness—Padmini felt it was all a recollection from another life.

Change is the only thing that is constant. Every second was a timekeeper to the change that took place each moment. Just now there was the blush of daybreak on the horizon. And now, suddenly, the sky had again turned into a battleground of ominous clouds.

Extreme attachment to anybody finally leads to extreme indifference. The king's behaviour towards Padmini was no longer as warm as it used to be. His cold indifference was obvious to her. A man's attraction to a woman's beauty is perhaps just infatuation that turns into disenchantment with the passage of time.

A question, as sharp as a spear, pierced her. *What if I am handed over to the sultan?*

They call the women's apartment a harem. It is virtually hell, where women are kept as prisoners. Eunuchs and slave girls stand guard over them, and the sultan, suspicious by nature, comes to check his women's faithfulness. An inhuman life of unimaginable suffering.

Thoughts that portended a frightening future rendered her breathless. A feeling of foreboding weighed heavily on her, creating a disquieting stillness like the lull before a storm.

Quickly climbing the stairs, Sugna ran up to her. 'His Majesty, our *annadata,* is coming,' she panted. Out of breath, Sugna was a picture of nervousness; as if she knew that something ominous was in the offing. There was unusual commotion in every part of Padmini Mahal.

Padmini's heart began to pound as though it would jump out of her chest. Her bloodstream seemed to have changed its course. A strange restlessness took over her.

Then there was an announcement:

'Prithvi Raj Raj-Rajeshwhar Maharawal Ratan Singh is arriving!'

A few moments later, the maharawal walked in, his spine erect. Yet Padmini could detect the heaviness in his steps. Her heart sank. An unusual seriousness darkened his face. It was as if she had never seen him before. *Who was this stranger?* Padmini felt as if her life was hanging from a gibbet. Her mind went blank. She stared senselessly into space. She shifted by looking searchingly into his eyes, as if trying to read his mind. His expression was blank, unreadable. She kept trying to get him to look at her, to reach out to him wordlessly.

He kept avoiding her eyes.

Slowly, he came to the bed and sat on it, leaning on a bolster. He closed his eyes and remained still like one deep in meditation. It seemed as though he was, at that moment, battling a war of thoughts. What was it? Was it about the glorious past? Or was it about their grim future?

She walked up to him noiselessly and placed her hand on his shoulder. He opened his eyes as though he had come out of reverie. She looked at him again, cajoling him wordlessly with her eyes, seeking an answer.

For quite some time not a word was spoken.

'Why don't you say something?'

Her gentle query only made him more restless. Beads of perspiration appeared on his forehead. His lips were dry. He stared at her without speaking. A mysterious void showed in his eyes. He seemed to retreat again into an abyss of thoughtlessness.

'What happened in today's . . . ?' She couldn't bring herself to complete the question. Yet she had to prise out of him what had happened. What was the sentence against her? What was the decision?

'There's so much to say. But in an effort to tell you all, I won't be able to tell you anything,' he said. His voice sounded dry and distant. His face was as fathomless as a stone image behind a wisp of smoke.

A storm of emotions erupted in Padmini's mind. Sheer fright engulfed her. That and anger. Today she was not his 'Padme', his beloved, his sweetheart, or his soulmate, as he dotingly called her. *What is making him feel guilty? What is going on that he's not able to share with me?*

She trembled, fearing an ill omen. Once again, she searched his face, hoping to find an answer. He closed his eyes again and turned inward, self-absorbed and tormented. 'What is it that is preying on your mind, Rajan?' she asked in a low voice. He came out of his deep thoughts. 'Well,' he began, 'I don't quite know how to say it to you. It is not always easy to say the truth. At this moment, I am not in a stable state of mind.'

There was no enthusiasm or energy left in him. He was speechless, as though his ego was reproaching him, ripping his existence to shreds. All this only made Padmini more nervous. Her palms started to sweat. She began to feel a strange sensation in her legs.

'What is it that you can't find words for?'

Maharawal Ratan Singh was silent for a moment. Then he turned towards a wall and said, 'That devil Ala-ud-Din has desired to see you once. Not in person but through a mirror. After he has seen your reflection, he will go back with his contingent of soldiers.'

She was speechless. The words were out. There it was, the monster desire, in words. A sharp thorn pierced her heart. It made a tiny tear that grew, ragged and shredded her until she felt that it would kill her. Her face, usually as lovely as the lily flower, turned ashen, as if she had been visited by the shadow of death.

His words swirled around her. The king sat in deep despair, his head lowered, his insides churned up, as if the words that came out of him were not his. He sat still. He may have looked cast in stone, but his anguish was poisonous acid, eroding everything it touched.

Her mind stopped working. It felt as if some venomous substance was seeping into her blood. An excruciating pain ran through her body, leaving her mind numb. Time stood still. And then it passed. Her first words were raw with emotion. 'Rajan!' she uttered. She cast a line. Would he pick it up and reel her in? Would he rescue her?

'Huh?' He responded in a painful drawl and then kept quiet. He ran his hand over the bedspread. His wavering thoughts would not allow him to concentrate.

'How can you trust him? What if he does not go back after that?'

He broke his silence. 'No. He has given it in writing, in his royal edict, that in accordance with the agreement, and according to the holy order, this condition shall be implemented.'

'Don't you think it is a virtual surrender of Mewar?' She fixed her imploring eyes on his face, attempting to read his mind.

'I am aware of all aspects of the situation,' he said in an indifferent and slightly harsh tone.

'So, I have to . . . ?' Again, she couldn't bring herself to complete the sentence.

He kept quiet. But the question was hanging in the air, awaiting a reply.

Padmini's silence became an eloquent expression of her pent-up frustration. She waited. He could not, would not, respond. His silence led to anger welling up inside her. 'This will bring disgrace not only to me but to all of Mewar.'

He continued to stare into the distance. What was it that he could see and she couldn't, she wondered bitterly. She had, all along, been dreaming of living a life of self-respect. *A queen. Is this what is delivered to queens?* Her agitated mind began to revolt. When words become powerless, it is the eyes that say a lot. Ratan Singh saw something in his wife's eyes, which incensed him. He flew into a rage, 'Mewar is torn asunder and the Rawal king sitting on its throne remains a mute spectator. Is that what you want?'

But his voice lacked his natural self-assurance. There was no concern for dignity. His valour had dried up. The image of her husband as a fearless warrior and self-respecting king, which she had so assiduously preserved in her heart, was unceremoniously shattered.

His fingers are moving involuntarily. In his heart of hearts he knows that what is happening is not proper. What is wrong with him? Why is he unable to listen to his conscience? Why isn't he astonished at what has become of him? He is a king. He can fight a battle, lead his armies, challenge the enemy. After all, this is not the first time that he has had to face an enemy's invasion or a full-fledged war. Then why, oh why, is he becoming weak, powerless, self-pitying?

Padmini had nothing to say. It felt like hundreds of scorpions were stinging her at the same time. Her mind was filled with anger and revulsion for the king. He had lost his manliness, she felt. And what had happened to his pride? She took a deep breath and stood up. There was no point in sitting at his feet. There was no saviour here. She was being held ransom, and the head of an empire felt helpless enough to bow to it. She felt sucked into the endless darkness that was permeating her soul.

The tide of Ratan Singh's emotions abated. In a flash, all his anger turned into piteous helplessness. He looked at his silently angry wife ingratiatingly, held her hands, and pulled her towards him. He said, 'Padme! I cannot change the course of destiny. Life is not only that which we yearn for. At times, some things that we cannot imagine in our wildest dreams happen.'

The tone of his voice had touched the apex of self-pity and was about to melt, as though he was unable to find words to express his agony, as though he was hurtling deep down into an abyss in search of some truth.

'I've been ceaselessly fighting with myself. But now it seems I have lost sense and direction. I know I am forcing you into doing something improper and, thus, committing a sin. But what am I to do? I'm shell-shocked myself.'

It was all that he could manage to say, almost as if he were reproaching himself and questioning his manliness. He had been reduced to being guilt-ridden and despondent. Aggressiveness of thought and action had taken leave of him. His sensitive mind, caught in the fierce fight between the force of circumstances and the sense of righteousness, had become perturbed and unsteady. Exhausted to the core, he seemed to have turned inwards, looking for something.

'Had that impious sultan demanded gems and jewellery, elephants, horses or any material wealth, I would have readily given him all. But that devil has the audacity to eye our Ranivas, the queens' apartment, a repository of our honour. Tell me, Padme, how can the royal Guhil dynasty accept this?'

Never before had he been lowered in his own eyes. Padmini had never seen him so miserable. He had lost his natural effulgence. He seemed emptied, as if scooped out of his core, unable to rise to the occasion in this hour of crisis. He was lying motionless. Tears flowed from the corners of his eyes. He placed his trembling hand on Padmini's.

Female attendants appeared at the doorway. The king sat up. They began to prepare for the meal. They mopped the square marble floor that was patterned like a chessboard. A sheet of white linen was spread, on which they placed a *bajot*, a six-legged hexagonal chowki. Attendants rushed around to serve the king and his consort. A large gold *thaal* was placed on the *bajot* and a *shat-rasa* meal—dishes of all six flavours were served.

The king opened his eyes slowly. He didn't feel like eating. 'I have no appetite,' he said.

Padmini was filled with anger and resentment, but for now she wanted him to eat his fill. 'All day you have been busy meeting your council of ministers and advisers. You didn't eat anything.' Persuasively, she requested him to eat.

Without saying a word, he unwillingly pushed a few morsels into his mouth, out of respect for the god of food. He sipped water from the palm of his hand, rinsed his mouth briefly, and got up. Deterred by his stern visage, she didn't feel encouraged to say anything. That he showed unwillingness to eat was not unexpected. Ever since the fort had been besieged, he would eat just a little as a formality.

Earlier, when he would sit down to eat, he would invariably offer her a bowl from his plate, asking her to partake of it as a gesture of love and respect. It was much later that she learnt about the gesture being in accordance with tradition. Today, none of that had happened.

She offered him a *tambul,* a betel leaf, mixed with a crystal of camphor and covered with gold foil. He kept it aside instead of eating it.

The attendants took away the thaal. The linen, the bajot, the serving bowls, the vessels and the ewers were deftly removed too.

Chand brought in the jug of wine and metal cups, arranged them on a table and left. Padmini closed the door and sat close to the king.

Both of them were lost in thought, as though the sources from which their conversations flowed had dried up. Ratan Singh appeared to be physically and mentally disturbed. It was with great difficulty that he kept his emotions reined in. With his eyes closed, he kept lying on the opulent bed. Soon enough, he returned to the tangled web of his problems. At his wits' end, he downed tumbler after tumbler of wine in order to drown his mental agony and soothe his tormented conscience.

Chand had made the liquor very strong. Soon, the king was lost to the world.

Padmini's mind was a storm. *How could he have taken the stand he did?* She had tried to prevail upon him, but he would not listen. As soon as she would try to strike a conversation, he would either pick up the cup to drink or look the other way.

He continued to drink late into the night. His eyelids began to droop. Intoxicated, he pulled his beloved wife towards him and said, 'My love, I know you are angry with me. Please do not sit so sad and sullen. My most beautiful wife! This world, this life, is to be enjoyed. Come, take a swig or two of this wine. No, no, this is not wine. This is the elixir of life, a divine potion, which will satiate all your desires. What is life if not satiation of desires?'

His contrived jovial tone, however, could not bring any glint of mirth to his eyes. On the contrary, the streak of gloom in them deepened. The forced smile on his lips seemed to have emerged from a blind well. He managed to hold his beloved wife's chin, raised it slightly and looked into her eyes. All he could see was a blind path, desolate and deserted.

'Why do you mourn, Padme? Even the greatest ascetic could not resist the attraction of a woman's beauty. This devilish sultan is, after all, a despicable human. Forget about him. You are blessed with the glow of the sun, my dear! Come, let me hold you in a warm embrace. Enjoy this bliss and forget everything else.'

She didn't stir. She sat indifferent, away from the lure of his touch. Ratan Singh put his empty cup down and came close to her. The heavenly beauty of his wife stirred his desire. He held her tight in his arms and kissed her for a long time. Nestled in his embrace, she could feel that beneath his strong and powerful arms, his heart was crying incessantly. She could feel the pain in every part of his body. She knew that holding her in his arms eased his frayed nerves and lowered the heat of his humiliation.

He collapsed on the bed. His eyes felt heavy and soon he was deep in sleep. She could hear the low and steady sound of his breathing.

She rose from the bed and sat disdainfully near the quivering flame of the lamp. In its flickering, weak light she saw her faltering hopes. Tears coursed down her cheeks. She wiped them and took a deep breath. She could still feel the king's fast and warm breathing. She wanted to ask him so many things. Unfortunately, all her questions remained unanswered. Resting her face on her long and delicate hands, she looked at the king who was fast asleep. She was pained to find that Ratan Singh, whom she had assumed to be a brave warrior, a protector of his clan, his dharma, his great culture and an apostle of high ideals and virtues, had betrayed her trust.

Suddenly, she felt as if some shadowless figure, like an apparition, was moving about in the darkness. Raghav Chetan. She shuddered. She could hear his loud, derisive laugh. She looked around, but there was nobody. It was only a delusion; her mind playing tricks. This was not the first time that she had had such hallucinations. Of late, her thoughts had been muddled. When alone, she was often overtaken by such thoughts of him.

She was reminded of that fateful evening six to seven months back.

Mewar had always been the spiritual seat of the great acharyas, the spiritual preceptors of Jainism. In those days, Acharya Jinprabhusuri had visited Chittor. The revered monk was not just a scholar of the philosophy of Jainism. He was also a spiritual master who had reconciled various aspects of scriptural knowledge, paths of austerity and penance, literary sentiments and emotions, aesthetics and art. The central concern of his preaching and discourses was to spread the message of upholding the values of compassion, charity and good conduct in public life. In order to make his discourses more interesting, he frequently referred to mythology and folktales. His narration would leave the audience captivated. In those days, he was busy writing his well-known oeuvre, *Vividh Tirtha Kalpa*. The book included a special mention of the life and times during the reign of Ratan Singh's father, Maharawal Samar Singh.

Ratan Singh had deep reverence for his father. He used to collect important information about other states from the acharya who used to stay at Vatapradi, Anahilpatan, Stambhatirtha, Gopadri, among other places.

That day, Ratan Singh went to the resting place of Jain munis to meet the acharya and to listen to his words of wisdom.

From there, he went straight to Padmini Mahal. Earlier, the company of the acharya would make him happy. But that day, he returned with a heavy heart. He informed Padmini, 'The acharya had paid a visit to the court of Sultan Ala-ud-Din in Delhi.'

Normally, there would have been nothing unusual in this piece of information. Acharya Jinprabhusuri was a great scholar. He had the royal authorization to travel unobstructed through the length and breadth of the country. It was quite common for him to visit the courts of different kings. But the unusual seriousness with which this was conveyed indicated that something remained unsaid.

'What did he say?' Padmini asked out of curiosity.

'He said he saw Raghav Chetan demonstrating his *tantra vidya*, his mysterious occult powers, in the court of the sultan of Delhi who appeared quite impressed. Also, he told the sultan something more.'

'What did he tell him?' she asked apprehensively.

'That the queen of Chittor, Rani Padmini, is the real *Padmini*, the most beautiful woman. No woman in the sultan's harem can come anywhere close to her in beauty and charm . . .'

She could understand that Raghav Chetan had said so out of malice. Furious with him for his dubious activities, the Rajan had reprimanded him severely. She had never liked him when he was part of the court. His words had sounded hollow and insincere to her. She hated the sight of him. She recalled how obsequiously and villainously he grinned, showing his buck teeth.

The Rawal king was quiet. Perhaps he had realized that in a fit of anger, he had made a mistake and that Raghav would avenge the mistreatment.

Padmini shut her eyes. Her breathing was quick and shallow. Raghav. She had a bad feeling about him from the time he had stepped into her life. She could summon his face in her head by just remembering his name: tonsured head, his ears covered with stiff hair, his shaggy eyebrows joined together, bags under his eyes . . . he had looked like a shabby tramp. Accomplished in the art of chicanery, sycophancy and hypocrisy, he used to hang around the maharawal day in and day out, toadying to him. He used to talk with the pretence of humbleness. She had never liked his dramatics, his immodest self-publicity, his taking recourse to gratuitous overstatements and rhetoric. There was something about him that made her dislike him, yet the maharawal was completely won over.

A person who is about to meet his doom is left with blunted wisdom.

He was considered to be the one most dear to the maharawal, but not many liked him. But, as they say, God will not be pleased until the guru is propitiated. So, because the maharawal was obviously besotted with Raghav, many of the courtiers began to treat him with respect.

From that time on, 'talent' began to be defined in a different context. Discrimination between man and man, ostentation, hypocrisy and arrogant show of knowledge became the values to be associated with it. Even the king was getting mired in misconceived notions. He started neglecting the affairs of the state and began to wallow in the luxuries and indulgences of palace life.

The throne of the state is not a bed of roses. The Turks had already been eyeing Mewar, but the king had conveniently buried his head in the sand and allowed himself to be surrounded by flatterers and sycophants.

His indulgence proved so fatal that his physical and mental strength, his courage and his fortitude began to dwindle. Sitting in Delhi, Sultan Ala-ud-Din continued to strike here and there at will. But Ratan Singh kept his eyes and ears closed, feigning ignorance. His ambition began to lose much of its fire and he was not as vigilant as he used to be. As a result, the enemy had moved stealthily enough to breathe down their necks. Instead of facing the situation bravely, the king seemed to be looking for an escape route.

Padmini harboured strong resentment and bitterness against Ala-ud-Din. That he had the audacity to put forth a humiliating proposal to the king of Mewar was despicable.

Yet, she did not have to do much soul-searching to know that her anger towards Ratan Singh was far more intense.

In those days, no courtier or adviser was as close to the king as Raghav Chetan. He had won the king's trust in full measure. He was a *tantrik* who had come from another state and was known to have acquired supernatural powers. Earlier, he had already impressed Raja Ram Dev, the king of Devagiri, with his mysterious skills. He was a sorcerer and had described his tantra vidya to Ratan Singh in great detail.

He had told the king that in tantra, the ritualistic puja is aimed at the discovery of invisible powers of the universe by means of the hidden potential of man's body and mind. The principal deities of the tantriks are Shakti, Shiva and their attendants. In tantra vidya theory, their forms are different from those commonly imagined. According to its philosophy, the Kundalini Shakti, or the serpent force, lies coiled in a dormant state in the Sushumna nerve of the spinal column. There are invisible chakras signifying energy centres in different points of our body. This dormant kundalini can be awakened by performing a devotional practice prescribed in the tantra. Once it is awakened, the practitioner can possess supernatural powers.

He also told the king that the temples of the practitioners of tantra had no roofs because they performed their puja under the open sky.

Raghav Chetan used to resort to sorcery prescribed in the tantrik practice at a secluded spot and in complete silence. Apart from being a practitioner of *mantra sadhana*, he was a scholar of Sanskrit. He wrote two books in Sanskrit in which his poetic compositions were steeped in the *shringar rasa* or erotic sentiment. It was he who had once told the Rajan that according to ancient texts on eroticism, women had been divided into four categories in accordance with their physical charm and erotic appeal—Padmini, Chitrani, Hastini and Survani. A Padmini, rated the best, is delicate, good-natured, courteous and very beautiful. He quoted a Sanskrit verse:

> *Padminī padmagandhā cha, pushpagandhā cha chitranī*
> *Hastinī madyagandhā cha, matsyagandhā cha survanī*
> *Padminī suryavadanī, chandravadanī cha chitranī*
> *Hastinī kamalavadanī, kāk vadnī cha survanī*

A Padmini is fragrant like a lotus; a Chitrani is scented like a flower; a Hastini is aromatic like an intoxicating substance, and a Survani smells like a fish. A Padmini's body has the effulgence of the sun; a Chitrani's body has the luminescence of the moon; a Hastini has the pinkish complexion of a lotus; and a Survani has the dark complexion of a crow.

Padmini never appreciated such classification of women, nor did she like such elaborate descriptions of each and every part of a woman's body. She considered it indecent.

She deprecated this male chauvinism that allowed a man to judge the elegance of a woman's body from the standpoint of his erotic mindset. Why is womanhood not seen in its totality—her absolute loyalty to her husband, her sense of dedication, tolerance, her feelings of love and affection? Why doesn't he understand that the beauty of a woman is not confined to her body but that it transcends to her mind and soul. He should know that every woman is a beauty, specific to her individuality and, therefore, all women cannot be flocked or herded together in such groups.

The realization in a woman that there is somebody who is deeply attached to her and loves her intensely creates a beauty that makes her attractive and charming. A feeling that somebody is infatuated with her adds grace and elegance to her personality. It is true that elegance is rooted in beauty. But beauty has several dimensions: beauty of body, beauty of mind, beauty of temperament, beauty of values inherited, beauty of the spirit to struggle on. Feelings are inextricably linked with the beauty of a woman.

A man's ego doesn't allow him to know this, and even when he knows it, he doesn't respect a woman's feelings as he finds it unmanly.

The name that she was given had a traditional belief attached to it. She was named Padmini after consulting learned priests.

The word 'padmini' means not only a beautiful woman but also an assemblage of lotus flowers. But who would explain this to the maharawal . . . he was rather impressed by Raghav's poetic language steeped in erotic sentiment. Raghav Chetan, meanwhile, took full advantage of this proximity to the king. He was talkative and impertinent. Besides, the privilege of being the king's right hand earned him many benefits.

Men were barred from entering the women's apartment in the palace, but Raghav had contrived the king's permission to visit it without restrictions. Riding his high horse, he would contemptuously bluff his way past all guards. He considered talking to the palace guards beneath his dignity.

Almost everybody in the palace and the court was unhappy with him for his duplicitous conduct, but nobody dared say anything for fear of incurring the king's wrath. If anybody had the courage to question him, it was Gora Rawat, a brave warrior. He had perhaps sensed that Raghav was more dangerous than a cobra, and if nothing was done to check him urgently, he would spew his venom on someone. But there is no knowing when a king, a yogi, fire or water will be pleased with you and treat you kindly; just as there is no way of knowing when they could turn around and be hostile.

The stand Gora took against Raghav cost him dearly and he was suspended from the services of the state.

Padmini could vividly picture the entire incident.

That day, all preparations for hunting had been made. There was a place in Ahar village where the Berach flowed through the vast mountain range and descended on the plains. Nature's beauty was in abundance there. It was a wildlife habitat. The Rajan had made up his mind to go hunting and also wander about in the woodland. His soldiers had already arrived.

Before setting out, the king had visited Padmini in her room to take his leave of her. He had just taken her into his arms and held her face affectionately, when suddenly, his eyebrows arched, his eyes became stern and his face turned stony.

'Ra . . . gha . . . v!' he thundered. His loud and angry voice rocked the atmosphere, breaking the words into pieces.

Taken aback, Padmini turned around and saw Raghav. He must have been peeping and had not expected to be spotted. Caught red-handed, he seemed shaken. The dazed expression on his face flickered like the severed tail of a lizard.

'How dare you!' Enraged by Raghav's insolence, the king ground his teeth, his hands clenched into fists and his lips quivering.

Nervously, Raghav shifted his stole from one shoulder to the other absent-mindedly. He had been very close to the king and knew his nature well. Never before had he seen the Rajan so furious. Frightened by the blazing fury in the king's eyes, he lost his silver tongue. His face fell. He realized the gravity of his misconduct. Despite that, or perhaps because of it, he seemed completely drained of the courage to seek forgiveness. All his erudition, knowledge, his pretended *vairagya* or asceticism vanished instantly.

The maharawal was wild with rage. His eyes turned red and his jaw was clenched. Nobody had known the Rawal king to tremble with fury. Their hearts shuddered with apprehension.

'Throw this rascal out!' he ordered the palace guards. His voice took on the pitch of uncontrollable anger. Two palace guards came forward and held Raghav tightly on either side. Raghav stood paralysed. This unexpected aggression had left him smouldering. His face had turned red.

As Raghav was escorted out, Padmini caught a perverse glint of vengeance in his eyes. It was a momentary flicker and then the calm façade was back on his face. Padmini stood aghast at the theatrics she had glimpsed.

Even after the tantrik had left, the king's eyes had continued to blaze with anger. She was stunned to see his body tremble with rage and his eyes turn bloodshot. The attendants exchanged fearful looks and scurried away. The entire women's apartment seemed to tremble with fear.

Later they learnt that Raghav had fled to Delhi with all his ignominy, apprehending that he might be thrown into the underground cell. There he contrived to gain access to the sultan's court.

It was he who, by repeatedly describing Padmini and her rare beauty to Sultan Ala-ud-Din, nurtured and inflamed his carnal desires. Raghav did it with a single-minded purpose. He wanted to avenge his humiliation by creating circumstances under which Padmini would be forced to become Ala-ud-Din's courtesan.

Who could have imagined that such a minor incident in her life would blow up to such horrible proportions? Thoughts of impending disgrace, anguish and indignation riddled her heart. She got up and stood near the window.

The growing darkness engulfed everything. She stared into space with intense sadness and grief crowding her mind.

The cosmos is endless in its expanse. Countless galaxies of stars and planets are spread over it. Varun, the god of the sky, makes the sky move. Clusters of these celestial bodies are his eyes, with which he closely watches what everybody is doing.

'Can't you see the cruelty and wickedness of the sultan, Lord Varun? I don't understand the mystery of your divine law,' she said aloud, looking at the sky, appealing to the celestial Varun.

It was past midnight when the Rajan woke up with a hangover. He had sobered up, but he was not completely awake. His eyes, red because of the storm whirling inside his head, looked drained and droopy. He scrunched up his eyes and looked around in dismay but stayed in bed in a semi-conscious state. It looked as though he was flailing about at the bottom of the sea. In between waking up and dozing off, he seemed to look at things as though they were phantasmagorical.

He rose to his feet, but felt giddy. He tried to walk a few steps but stopped when he began to stagger. He managed to come close to Padmini and stared at her. The mad look in his eyes and the helpless restiveness on his face made her sob. She burst into tears. He didn't try to console her. Instead, he stood as motionless as a rock. The room was drowned in suppressed silence. He tried to speak through his eyes, 'Dear Padme! Bear this pain for a short while. This is the last attempt.'

He looked pathetic, as though he were a weak and unprotected child. Suppressing her anguish, she bowed her head.

I have to bear this pain. I don't want my husband to feel that I intend to disobey him. If he wants me to undergo this suffering for the good of Mewar, then so be it.

It made her heart ache. An all-powerful king diminished to this level of powerlessness! What a cruel stroke of fate!

She had seen the king in an altogether different form. She wanted to beseech that form back: he with his head held high, his eyes lit up with a sense of pride; he who would not deign to look anywhere below the top of the mountain. There was nobody around who could have stood before the brilliance of his valour. Where was that king?

Holding his stole in one hand, the king staggered out, refusing to meet her eyes. Her heart was filled with both anger and pity for him. The long history of Mewar's pride and glory was coming to an end. She wanted to cry.

The cruel night had passed and she was, with her hands extended, begging for a ray of light. Her hope, the king, had walked away instead of standing by her. The morning was lost on her.

The pressure of apprehension, fear and its tremor continued to grow in her. On the shelf was a copy of *Shrenika Charitra*, an epic written by Acharya Jinprabhusuri. She took up the book and started reading it to mitigate her fear. It was her favourite book; one she had read a couple of times.

The epic, consisting of eighteen cantos, described the life and times of Maharawal Shrenik. He was a legendary hero characterized by the qualities of gallantry, chivalry, valour and noble conduct. Since it had the aspects of both grammar and characterization in epic proportions, it was also known by another title: *Durgavrittidayashraya*.

The epic poem was so powerful that the reader was irresistibly drawn to it and transported to a world of blissfulness. The entire epic was replete with the most hallowed traditions of righteousness, with even a casual reading offering a sense of peace and tranquillity. Each canto was titled according to the incident it described and ended with a brief reference to the next storyline.

The acharya, its author, was a scholar of grammar and philosophy.

The king was a connoisseur of art and literature. He relished discussions on the art of poetry. He was deeply impressed by the poetic maturity and erudition of the acharya and would speak glowingly about how the author had presented his scholarship so lucidly.

Padmini opened the book and started reading a benedictory verse while remembering Rishabhanatha.

Siddhau varnāsamāmnāyah sarvasyopachikīrshatā
Yenādau jagade Brahmna yen nandyānnabhinandana

She started brooding again. *One thinks and plans, yet what ultimately happens is different. I had my own dreams and imaginations . . . Where have they all gone now?*

At one point, she had a future planned. She had thought of donating some money to charity and getting beautiful temples constructed, thus spending the rest of her days working for the well-being of those in need.

Likhvanbai had once told her that Jayatalli Devi, the maharawal's grandmother, was so impressed by the discourses of a Jain scholar of Gachcha that she got the Shyam Parshwanath temple constructed there. Later, her son, the Rajan's father, had donated a plot of land to Pradyumna Suri, the acharya of Gachcha, for a monastery to be set up.

She had heard about the generosity and broad-mindedness of Rajmata Jayatalli Devi, who, despite being a devotee of Lord Shiva, had made a donation for the construction of Jain temples. Likhvanbai had shown her the gift-deed inscribed on a copper plate, which she had borrowed from the museum. Having seen the names of those who donated large sums written on copper plaques, Padmini instantly yearned to see her name on one of them, with *'Shri Ganeshaya Namah'* written on top or one mounted on the Chunda's spear. The coming generations would remember her just like Mata Jayatalli Devi.

Alas, that was not to be. Her mental agony weighed heavily on her. The part of her mind that stored her lofty ambitions began to empty. She kept sitting for a long while, downhearted, confounded and lost. To be left before a debauched sultan, by transgressing the bounds of morality, is an indelible blot on the glorious reputation of this royal dynasty, she thought.

It will break me completely. I won't be able to stand it. That moment will be unbearable. No, I want mukti, salvation from this ignoble life.

Padmini groaned in anguish, 'O Krishna! Where are you? You made possible what was an impossible task by salvaging the honour of Draupadi in a courtroom full of men. And here you are not listening to my prayers.'

Finally, the cursed moment arrived in all its ferocity. All preparations had been made in the main corridor. Lavish arrangements and the display of opulence were at their peak.

Gifts had been placed on large round plates: *khilat*, a robe of honour especially designed for the sultan; gem-studded armour and ornaments; ruby and emerald rings; gold coins, both *asharfi*s and *mohar*s; and expensive shawls. Nobility and officers were also given precious gifts according to their status.

Yet, the grandeur was only a thin cover. The palace, fragrant with the variety of dishes being prepared, was unable to mask the fear that roiled in its interiors. The air crackled with tension.

The stifling silence was drowned in the mist of uncertainty. The light from everyone's eyes had been extinguished. They had fallen silent as though they had committed a crime. Life looked like a desert, desolate, where every drop of water had dried up.

Padmini sat still, scared. As the fateful hour came closer, her fear grew. Her hands and feet turned cold. Her forehead was wet with cold perspiration. She began to see yellow particles flying before her eyes. Her heart began to palpitate.

'Patience, Ranisa,' said Sugna. She placed her hand gently on Padmini's back, trying to console her.

But whatever patience she had was gone. What was left was an unbearable burden, which continued to grow. Could one have patience at a moment of facing an odious beast ready to pounce on its prey, and the moment of stripping naked one's soul? She shut her eyes and tried to stay afloat in the darkness.

The inauspicious hour had arrived.

Sugna breathed, 'Please come, Ranisa!'

She felt as if she was being pushed from the peak of a hill into a deep gorge. She was falling helplessly.

The all-powerful royal dynasty of the Guhils, which had always trounced its enemies, whose reputation transcended all boundaries, had to face this ignominy. They were forced to send their queen, who had not been touched even by the sun, before the brutal Ala-ud-Din. The shining glory of all past victories stood tarnished this day.

She was hurt, humiliated and wallowing in soiled modesty. Agony had stressed all her nerves. Her hands turned icy cold. A shiver, rising from her fingers, ran through her entire body. She began to tremble like a dried leaf. The ground under her feet seemed to cave in. The sky overhead seemed to approach her menacingly as if to devour her.

Blue waves of deadly poison were lapping against her.

Her throat was dry, her feet were faltering, and her vision was blurred. An unbearable pain caused restlessness; pressure built up in her temples. With every step, she felt her energy ebbing away. She dragged herself like an innocent animal being taken to the sacrificial altar. Following her were her attendants, who were walking mechanically, as though under a spell. An unfathomable pain had settled in their eyes.

By the time she reached the appointed venue, she had almost fainted. She looked as though she was lifeless.

A death-like shadow had spread all around. Everybody's self-esteem, their feelings of dynastic pride were blown to bits.

More insightful now, Padmini became aware of her position. The king, the Ranas, the entire royal family, the feudal chieftains, the retainers, the guards and the attendants had vanished. If there was anything left behind, it was the awareness that she was alone.

She was seated close to an oriel adorned with precious gemstones, her reflection clearly visible in a large mirror. She looked completely absorbed in herself, her face frozen. She kept her eyes closed so that she would not have to look at that devil by mistake. As she faced the most demeaning moment of her life, Rani Padmini perhaps looked more beautiful than ever. An unusual loveliness had covered her gloomy face.

Even with her eyes closed she could sense a pair of lustful eyes peering at her like a customer evaluating goods at a shop. It numbed her senses and left her petrified.

Her forehead was damp. A frightening moment of impending death seemed to have stayed forever. Everything lay exposed in that cruel heartless glare. The ego had been trampled underfoot, and a severely wounded moment had blown all ideals to smithereens. She felt as if her head was being hit with a hammer.

Black lines of gloom started streaming out of a hitherto unblemished block of ice. Very soon, the glory of beauty began to fade because of the unchecked trauma. On the verge of losing consciousness, Padmini felt bereft of her remaining strength; as though there was nothing left in that paralysed body.

A painful contortion rising from her stomach wrenched her heart terribly. Her legs began to tremble. A ball of smoky wind began to spin inside her. Black, round spots began to swim in front of closed eyes. Her head was throbbing.

She was about to faint. Her attendants rushed to help. Her mind was filled with feelings of guilt and remorse as though she had committed a grave sin. It left a bitter taste in her mouth.

All her royal pride and ego fell to pieces.

* * *

Padmini was lying on her bed, motionless. On either side, her attendants waved hand-held fans lightly. That cursed moment had passed like a scary nightmare. Every moment she lived, every breath she took was as painful as being bitten by a thousand snakes.

She gasped for breath. Sugna spritzed her face with cold water and then wiped it softly. A few drops of the medicine prescribed by the *raj vaidya*, the royal physician, were put into her mouth. Slowly, she gulped and let out a feeble moan of pain. Something extremely bitter spread in her mouth.

She looked as though she had been ill for years. Sugna dipped her head, almost touching her ear, and uttered softly, 'Ranisa.'

Her face fluttered a little, but her eyelids did not open. Adding all the love and affection to her voice, Sugna repeated, 'Ranisa!'

Padmini regained some consciousness. She had to gather all her strength to raise her fragile eyelids. Slowly, she came to her senses. With some effort she was able to open her eyes. Her gaze was steady, but there was nothing in them to indicate that she had any interest in living. There was no flame of desire of any kind in them. She made an attempt to say something, but her voice trembled like a flickering flame and then fell silent.

Her lissome body looked emaciated and bloodless. It was as if there was no life left in her. That she had been disgraced in public view filled the innermost depths of her heart with voices of self-condemnation and disgust.

Sugna's hand was caressing her back. Her affectionate touch gave Padmini much-needed comfort. She felt consoled and reassured. She was coming out of the state of inertness slowly, but steadily. Memories of persons and places were coming back, which helped her manage the pain to an extent.

'How do you feel now?' Sugna asked tenderly.

Padmini swivelled her head weakly, her face devoid of emotions. It looked as though an ocean had dried up, and beautiful flower beds had turned into islands of sand. Her parched lips quivered, 'I'm all right.'

She gestured that she needed to be by herself. Sugna asked the other attendants to leave. She sat at Padmini's feet and with one hand began to stroke the sole of her foot.

The room was still submerged in guilty silence. Those hideous moments had stayed in her thoughts, as though they had been branded in her mind with a red-hot iron rod. That heart-wrenching pain had come alive once again. Her heart began to ache inconsolably. She felt as if a soundless scream was trapped in her throat. Her face had lost its glow.

Somewhere within, she had assumed that her strong devotion to god would have prevented this from happening; and that if it did happen, it would enable her to overcome this agony. That faith of hers now stood shaken. All her prayers made in solitude had gone unanswered. For the first time in her life, she realized the futility of her devotional practices.

The door of the room was ajar. There was a scramble of voices outside. The attendants were chatting. Snatches of their conversation could be heard inside. It was Magan's voice they heard first.

'How awful he looked! There was nothing sultan-like in him.'

Lakshmi, who had a discerning eye for looks and demeanour, said, 'How gaudy and garish was his apparel! He was not just wearing gems and jewels but was literally dripping with them.'

'How shamelessly he was leering at one attendant after another, taking each of them to be the queen!' It was Chand's voice.

'How brutish his eyes were, blood-red with heavy drinking! Far from a king, he looked as if he was an uncivilized, uncultured ruffian.'

'Not just uncultured but a demon in human garb. When he laughed, his ugly, dirty and unshapely large teeth would stick out.'

'Did you notice how greedily he was gawking at Ranisa? It looked as if his eyes would pop out.'

'Did you see Raghav Chetan?'

'Yes, yes.' Many voices came together.

'He was constantly whispering in Ala-ud-Din's ear.'

'Ungrateful!'

'Listen, Magan! Where are you going?'

'The old badaran, the lady caretaker, has called me. The main kitchen is being purified with water from the Ganga.'

'Stop talking, girls!' Sugna came out of the room to scold the attendants who were chatting non-stop.

Instantly, everybody fell silent.

Just then the old woman, the badaran, came beating her breast and crying loudly. Watching her run in with panic, everybody grew agitated, knowing instinctively that something inauspicious had happened. The old woman looked terrified; her face was white with fear. All eyes were on her.

Hearing the commotion, Padmini appeared in the doorway. Sensing something untoward, she was overcome by an unknown fear. With her heart in her mouth, she watched the scene helplessly.

'Those devils have held the annadata hostage. They have taken him away to their camp,' said the old woman.

'What nonsense is this old woman talking? Has she gone senile?' All of them looked at her quizzically.

One of them approached her and asked apprehensively, 'They have taken our annadata to the enemy camp as a prisoner? Are you sure about what you are saying?'

'Yes, yes. I saw it with my own eyes,' the old woman gasped.

'What?' Their jaws dropped.

An ominous silence descended, as though a thunderbolt had hit them.

Chhagan mustered up the courage and asked her, 'What were our brave soldiers deputed for the king's security doing?'

'They were taken by surprise. The sultan's men played a dirty game. They gained entry into the fort deceitfully on the pretext of seeing around the palace. All of a sudden, they surrounded the king, to the consternation of all.'

She was crying inconsolably. 'What more is in store for us? These Turks have caused havoc.'

Before the people of Mewar could fully recover from the disgrace, here was another blow. Their mouths dried up. They felt as though both earth and sky had been shattered.

The old badaran fell to Padmini's feet and wept bitterly. 'Those demons have destroyed all our peace and happiness,' she said raising her head skywards. She wailed, 'God! What is this will of yours? Why do you want us to suffer this pain and disgrace?'

Everybody was in a state of shock and dismay. Magan collapsed. Covering her eyes with her hands, she started howling. Chand and Nanhu stood speechless. Sugna, not knowing what to do or say in this hour of crisis, looked helplessly at the old woman and at Padmini. She could not bring herself to believe what had happened.

The old woman was weeping unstoppably. She raised her callused hands and began to curse the enemy, 'May complete ruination befall you. I curse you. You will be remembered by all only as an odious devil. Your own power will bring your annihilation. You and your entire clan will perish with no one left behind to take your name. You will suffer the worst punishment in hell, while you are living.' Her words, screaming, curses, were swirling in the air.

'He is a pervert with the brain of a beast,' said Chhagan. Her voice was choked with rage.

Their eyes were void of expressions of hope.

A small group of attendants approached Padmini. None of them had the nerve to say a word.

The shocking news struck Padmini like a thunderbolt. For a while, all she could hear and feel was the tingling in her brain and the beating of her heart. Nonplussed, unconscious of her surroundings, petrified, she stood transfixed in the doorway as if she were a statue. And then she fell.

* * *

It took her some time to regain consciousness. Pain had blinded her and enveloped her in a bubble of harsh silence. She was about to lapse into unconsciousness again, but she pulled herself together with effort. It seemed like it was the end of life and she was on the brink of death.

Everybody was at their wits' end, wondering how to console her and what to say to assuage her torment.

Bewildered and blinded by deep melancholy, she muttered to herself: They have held the Rajan captive by deceit. But why? Why did they do so? Hadn't he agreed to the sultan's conditions? It was his proposal and the Rajan had complied with it. What happened all of a sudden?

It was he who had come with this treaty. How can a person who claims to be the Sultan of Delhi stoop so low as to go back on his word? How is it that he didn't think twice before hatching the most abominable conspiracy? Didn't his conscience condemn him? He had sworn on his Iman, his Faith. This deceitful conduct of the sultan was a ruthless betrayal of all canons of justice, ethics, morality and even manliness. How unreasonably and uncannily the cycle of events had turned. What's going on, and where would it end?

A stunned silence prevailed; the city and the palace were completely desolate.

She didn't know when Sugna left the room. When she returned, her eyes were full of tears. Her face was pale. She was trying, unsuccessfully, to look up and hide her tears.

Padmini was alarmed by an impending sense of doom. She looked at Sugna apprehensively. She sensed bad news.

'Tell me, Sugna, what has happened?' It was with great difficulty that she brought herself to ask this question.

Sugna covered her face with her odhani.

Why is she silent? Why doesn't she speak? Her anxiety had reached its climax and could no longer be suppressed. She came close to Sugna and uncovered her face, which was drenched in tears. 'The sultan has sent an emissary with his royal edict,' Sugna sobbed. Her voice was drowned in sobs. Her throat constricted and she covered her face again.

'What has he said?' asked Padmini harshly.

It was probably the sternness in her tone that compelled Sugna to uncover her face. Still, she needed some effort to say what she had left unsaid. 'The edict states that if Rani Padmini is given over to the sultan, he will place all the comforts and luxuries of the world at her feet and set Maharawal Ratan Singh free. After this has been done, he will lift the siege and remove his encampment. But if this condition is unacceptable to the king, then . . .'

'Then what? What will he do? Why don't you tell me?' Padmini asked with uncontrollable anguish in her voice.

The melancholy in Sugna's eyes deepened further. 'In that case, he will kill the king and attack Chittor.'

Dumbstruck, Padmini felt the words 'Kill the king' echoing all around and assaulting her ears continuously. A corroding pain ran through her body and mind.

A disconsolate Sugna held her hand. 'At this difficult juncture,' she said, 'you have to have some courage and patience. It is with patience that you can overcome this crisis.' She couldn't say anything more and fell silent. Tears kept flowing from her eyes.

Padmini didn't stir and kept sitting meditatively with her eyes closed. It looked as though she had turned into a rock that didn't know how to melt and flow.

Unnoticed, Lakshmi entered and stood there. With trepidation, Padmini asked, 'What have they decided to do?'

'They are still in consultation. They've not arrived at any decision yet. The advisory council is holding a meeting. Veerbhan, the crown prince of Mewar, is attending it.'

Just then Magan came running in. All eyes turned to her with irrepressible curiosity. She must have some special message to convey, they surmised. She was panting.

Lakshmi asked her impatiently, 'What news have you brought? Tell us, we can't wait. I'm on the verge of collapsing.'

'I don't know exactly what transpired. But . . .' she gasped for breath.

Apprehending some bad news, Sugna walked up to her and asked, 'But what?'

'They are likely to succumb to the sultan's threat and surrender Ranisa to him.' Her voice faltered as she tried to convey the most devastating message. Tears coursed down her face.

Sugna's eyes flooded with tears. She tried her best to say something but failed. Her throat and lips ran dry.

Padmini was outraged. Impotent wrath brought tears to her eyes.

What do they take a wife to be? Do they think that a wife is a commodity which can be given over to anybody just like that? Is she so inferior and contemptible? Why is her status as a woman subject to insults and humiliation time and again? Why, oh why? She searched the remotest corner of her mind but could find no answer to her question.

Her question was moving in circles, like ripples created when a stone is dropped into water.

The cycle of her thoughts started spinning faster and would not stop. She was faced with a strangely menacing predicament. On the one hand there was the safety and security of the king and the kingdom of Chittor, and on the other, her honour, dignity and chastity were at stake.

Overcome with grief, anger and humiliation, she thought of killing herself.

But will this save the life of the maharawal, the king? Will this stop death and destruction in Chittor?

A furious storm raged inside her, leaving her agitated and disturbed. Her mind was buzzing with the Rajan's cries for help, as though he was being whipped mercilessly in the sultan's captivity. *He is in great distress. I cannot let him suffer this ordeal. I'll give up my life, my everything, to save him from torture.*

She had heard of the horrible conditions of the harems. Many of the wives and daughters of the sultan, and other women lodged there, had died of the suffocating inhuman treatment. The eyes of many so-called princesses had been plucked out. The sultan had put many of them to the sword. If she, too, were to be consigned to the same harem, then . . . ? She did not have the nerve to think beyond 'then'. But the question stood before her, unmoving like a hill.

With her nerves in tatters, she kept calling Sugna for something or the other; sometimes to fetch water, sometimes to shut the door, then to open a window. Sometimes she didn't remember why she had called her. Sugna could understand why she was behaving like this, but she couldn't find the words to console her.

The day segued into the evening.

The evening *aarti* that day was being performed in the Shri Eklinga temple. The sounds of the conch shell and bells were accompanied by the chanting of prayers.

The words and sound of the prayers reached out to her and offered immense solace. In their soothing strains, she began to feel a divine blissfulness.

Thanks to the strength of prayers, somewhere in a dark corner of her mind, the last glow of pride and self-esteem rose, flickering and refusing to die.

A large number of brave men from this royal family have laid down their lives to keep alive their pride and self-respect for centuries. How can their supreme sacrifice be allowed to go waste? How can they let their glorious history be wiped out from the face of this earth in one stroke?

She tried to collect her dwindling courage and to calm her agitated mind and frayed nerves.

For a while she kept sitting there, with absolutely no thought in her mind.

Something will have to be done. I will not allow this unwise thing to happen. First of all, I'll have to overcome this despondency and this defeatist mentality. A mind full of pessimistic thoughts cannot give anyone any hope. I am all alone, helpless and insecure. Unless this depressing feeling is conquered, no new idea can arise in my mind. Something or the other will have to be done. The way out of this predicament is within me. It is inside. But what is that something? Where is it? In what form?

She had no identifiable thought. But *some* idea had been born.

The entire palace was submerged in a depressing silence. Sugna came in with a lamp stand, which she placed on its affixed base. The ring of light created an aureole around itself while the rest of the room was blanketed in indefinable darkness.

Sugna approached Padmini with light steps and said, 'Prince Veerbhan will be here any moment. He'll convey to you the message from the parishad.'

Veerbhan? It's been ages since I last saw him. And what message is he coming with?

Her mind was lashed by waves of all kinds of wild guesses. Her faith, once again, began to wobble. She felt as if she was standing all alone on the brink of a deep and dark gorge.

With some trepidation, she braced herself to receive the message.

A sense of impending doom gripped her. It was beyond her imagination how she would take that ominous message. Despite the chill in the air, her brow was beaded with perspiration.

Collecting all her strength and wisdom, she tried to calm her perturbed mind. Inside, she felt tremendous disquiet, but no one could have fathomed as much by looking at her poised demeanour.

Sugna entered again and informed her that the prince had arrived.

Her heart raced. Showing restraint in her voice, she said, 'Show him in.'

Prince Veerbhan came unaccompanied. Some years ago, when she had first met his mother, she had caught a glimpse of him. Now, she took a good look. He had grown into a strapping young man. But his face still retained the unblemished innocence of youth. Like his father, he was tall with broad shoulders; he had a fair and prominent forehead, a long, sharp nose and attractive eyes.

A feminine glow on his face was reminiscent of his mother, Queen Prabhavati. A closer look revealed that he needed some more hard work and military exercise. A subtle sense of distress had mellowed his aristocratic upbringing as a Kshatriya.

His gem-studded armlet was gleaming in the light of the lamp. There was an innocent artlessness on his face. Suddenly, Padmini felt a surge of motherly love. *How fortunate is his mother!*

The prince bowed to her respectfully. Padmini surveyed him with all the calmness and dignity she could muster. 'Welcome, Prince!' There was neither entreaty nor an order in her words. They were merely words; hollow, devoid of any feelings. 'Come and sit here.'

Veerbhan took his seat on a cushioned chair. He sat quiet, and the expression on his face was impenetrable. Padmini searched his eyes but was unable to read his mind.

Unaware of what was going on in Padmini's mind, Veerbhan kept sitting there without saying a word.

'What message have you brought, Prince?' She broke the ice. The confidence in her tone seemed to startle him, but he recovered quickly.

'After prolonged discussion and consultation, it has been decided that Rani Padmini be offered to the sultan as a gift.' His tone was extremely restrained and dry.

There was no trace of warmth or mellowness in his voice.

Padmini was not shocked. Nor was she agitated. Instead, she kept quiet, as though she already knew about the decision. A smirk flashed on her lips and disappeared the next moment. She kept gazing at Veerbhan. He remained expressionless. His nonchalance hurt her deeply. It was very painful for her to know that he lacked any emotional concern for her and that he was not kindly disposed towards her. She had never expected this. Whatever the reason, her heart wept.

But, no matter what she felt, she could not allow herself to break down in front of a younger person. With great effort, she managed to suppress her feelings. Sorrow filled in rapidly.

'Is this decision in keeping with the pride and self-respect of Mewar?' she asked. Rage slowly took over.

The question was so sudden that the prince didn't know how to respond. He dropped his eyes. He paused for a while and then said meekly, 'We do not have any other option. The enemy has come right at our doorstep and is challenging us to face the consequences.'

She heard him with impatience. Her face was red with irritation. She struggled to control her anger, which was growing by the moment. 'It is very surprising, unfortunate and shameful that, being the scion of the royal family of Mewar, your blood did not boil, you didn't feel outraged by such a hideous proposal.' His eye caught the flame of rage that flashed in her eyes.

The face of the prince darkened with shame. He was groping for something within him. Gathering all his strength, he said, 'I've already told you, Ranisa, we are left with no option. The enemy is very powerful and Chittor is a very small state for him.' After a brief pause, he added, 'Moreover, we cannot shut our eyes to the crashing defeat of Ranthambore at his hands.'

Her glowing visage retained the same expression as before.

'You are mistaken, Prince! Neither is Chittor small, nor is its strength less. It is your fear which is great. You may perhaps recall that Hamir of Ranthambore had not accepted servility under Ala-ud-Din's regime. He laid down his life but never admitted that he was weak and helpless. This cowardly thought never entered that intrepid king's mind. Ranthambore was smaller in size and strength, with limited manpower compared to Mewar.'

'What you say is true. I agree with you. But every truth is not practicable. We have practical and logistic difficulties that are insurmountable and . . .' His guilt-ridden voice was left hanging in mid-air.

'These so-called practical difficulties arise out of your own inability to face the situation. Only the weak and infirm come out with such excuses. This is not the path for the brave to tread on, Prince of Mewar!'

He kept quiet for a moment. Or was he tongue-tied? He did not have any answer to offer. The conversation between them paused. The prince had heard that his stepmother was always peaceful and wore a smile. He was not prepared for this aggressive posture. Here was a lady who obviously wore her pride high, had a fire burning inside her; was well-informed, and brave at heart.

In an effort to control the conversation, he said, 'You are being emotional and in total disregard of the facts facing us. In *rajneeti,* in dealing with the affairs of the state, there is no place for emotions.'

His remarks were intended to provoke her, but she refused to rise to the bait.

'I agree, Prince, that emotions weaken the tough decisions taken objectively in ruling the state. But this kind of emotionalism is in fact positive and, therefore, in it lies its strength. The patriotic consciousness or deep and abiding love for one's motherland does not have its roots in the intellect; its base is moral. Did you ever think what lasting impact your policy of abject surrender will have on the citizens of this state, whose trust you hold? The incident of this moment will become a precedent. The present draws inspiration from the past. It is a bridge between the past and the future.'

Her voice, which was initially calm and placid, became excited towards the end. Something about Veerbhan's attitude of pretentious bravery triggered an annoyance within her which she tried to check, but in vain.

Veerbhan wanted to cut short this conversation. He had not come prepared to defend the committee's decision. He had assumed that he would convey the decree to a meek queen and that would be it. Ill-equipped as he was to parry her attack, he had to respond. He spluttered, 'We have resisted to the extent that was possible. If you coolly mull over it, you will come to the conclusion that there's no other option available to us.'

The words were delivered in a cautious tone.

Padmini could sense why he was modulating his tone. The hidden intent gave her a rude shock. Still, she kept her tone as calm as possible. 'There's hardly any scope to mull over it, Prince! Until and unless you muster up enough courage to protect your honour by preparing yourself to make great sacrifices, you will continue to wallow in self-pity.' There was no trace of despair and helplessness on her face.

Defensively, Veerbhan took on a harsh and bitter tone. 'It is not mine alone. It was taken by the parishad unanimously. According to a long-standing tradition, decisions on crucial matters are taken in consultation with the king, the feudal chieftains, the nobles and distinguished members of civil society. History bears testimony to the fact that many a times some major decisions were taken by feudal lords, which the king had to respectfully accept. This adventurism of pushing the entire state to the brink of disaster for the sake of a woman cannot be a wise move.'

Every sentence from him created turmoil in her mind.

The use of the expression 'a woman' pierced Padmini deeply, as though she had been hit by a *shabdabhedi vaan*, a mythical arrow that follows the trajectory of a sound.

Is a woman next to nothing? Doesn't he realize that a woman carries with her an entire culture? She is the very source of ethos and progeny. She is the preserver of long-cherished morals, customs and values. The evildoers perish, but culture flows eternally. Will Veerbhan, with this mindset, be the one ruling this state?

Her eyes flashed with a multitude of emotions: anger, contempt, indignation, vigour, hurt and more. So much more.

With her sharp mind she could guess that Veerbhan's thoughts and actions were full of antipathy and prejudice against her. Whatever he was saying was perhaps a culmination of years of bitterness towards her. Rani Prabhavati was bent on avenging the loss of her sole influence and exclusive claim on the king. Perhaps she wanted to give full vent to the rancour, which she had been harbouring for years, by taking revenge on Padmini. What better opportunity could come her way than this?

The venom of vengeance in his voice inflicted a thousand wounds on her self-esteem. But outwardly, she remained unaffected. The strength of her self-confidence lent a determined tenor to her voice. 'You talk of traditions, Prince? So, let me know, is there any tradition that allows the daughters and daughters-in-law of the royal family to be given away so spinelessly for the sake of the wealth or territory of the state?'

The prince, the son of Rani Prabhavati, was about to say something, but the words that had welled up to his lips receded instantly. He, however, continued to give her a look of disdain and disregard.

Padmini continued in an even more strident tone, 'Listen, Prince! Now that you have forced me to speak up, let me tell you in plain words that even if you ignore all other things, you cannot afford to ignore the fact that I, Padmini, am the wife of the king of Mewar and not second to Maharani Prabhavati, your mother and his first wife.' She went red with rage.

Bringing her pitch down, she added, 'This is hardly the time or occasion to rake up the wrangle in the family. It is true that destiny has made me the cause of this crisis, but am I to blame for this? As fear is bad, so is ill will. We cannot find the right way out unless we break this vicious circle of action and reaction arising out of this love-hate tangle.'

Veerbhan was taken aback by her aggressive posture. He felt greatly embarrassed, as though it was he and his mother Prabhavati who were solely responsible for Padmini's fate. He was not prepared for this. He was under the impression that Padmini was very simple and unambitious, and with that image of her in his mind he had come to deliver the message. He had thought that he could sweet talk her into accepting the decision. In fact, he had not even imagined that he would have to do that. What he saw of her was beyond his wildest imagination. His sullen surprise was overtaken by his need to defend the stance he had conveyed.

'This is not a new thing for royal families. Raja Ram Chandra Deo, the Yadava king, married his daughter to Ala-ud-Din. But he was not excommunicated on that account. The Huna, the Shaka, the Kushana and other rulers, too, entered into marital relationships with the royal families of Aryavart. This custom is neither unknown, nor is it humiliating.'

She felt as if she had been slashed with the quickness of lightning. Her eyes, her cheeks, her forehead turned red with indignation. Affronted by his brazen retort, she felt aggressive and resolute in her conviction.

However, she said with subdued anger, 'I am not arguing for the sake of argument, nor do I agree with your assertion. Rani Padmini is the wife of the king of this land. She was duly married to him with all the ceremonies and rituals, including the seven bridal steps and circumambulation around the sacred fire. The sanctity of the institution of marriage must be upheld at all costs. In accordance with this sacrament, I happen to be your mother. Just think, if your mother Prabhavati were in my place and she were to be bargained over like this, would you still keep sitting with your hands folded, do nothing and let things take their course fearing defeat at the hands of your enemy? Will that stand of yours be just or right?

Is it what you would call your dharma? The circumstances may change, but the truth does not. The truth is like the sun, always shining despite everything.'

After a little pause she continued, 'The king is there to protect and propagate dharma and righteousness, and not let it be destroyed. If he cannot lay down his life fighting *adharma*, the evil forces, his life is worthless. Listen, Prince, the would-be ruler of this kingdom! Remember, empires are built and destroyed, victory comes and goes, but only those who are dedicated to their cherished values and uphold them in the face of the worst circumstances are the ones who live their lives truly. It does not matter who wins the war ultimately. What matters is who fought for freedom and self-respect. Only they are admired and adored in times to come.'

The admonitory tone in Padmini's voice became more pronounced. The reasons she put forth were not intellectual rhetoric. They were an outcome of her deep understanding of the prevailing situation and the knowledge she had imbibed in the natural course.

'Killing one's conscience is far more terrible than defeat on the battlefield. This body without soul or conscience is as good as dead. The guilt of losing your pride and glory will eventually burn you to ashes.'

Veerbhan felt slightly wounded. He was finding it more and more difficult to justify his assertions. He found himself torn between his mother's secret wishes suggesting an easy way out of the crisis and Padmini's strong stance against meek submission. But he tried his best not to expose his vulnerable position.

'I understand, but it remains a fact that many sovereign rulers have bowed down before the sultan,' Veerbhan said, his tone softer. The disdain with which he had initially addressed her had been extinguished. No longer could he speak to her with feigned unconcern as he had earlier. 'Whoever dared to make light of his immense power invited total destruction of their states and their people. In the circumstances, what else can we do?'

Is that all they could come up with? Annoyed at their helplessness, Padmini was furious. She realized that there was no use losing her temper or breath any more. Yet, she had to say, 'Don't tell me about his enormous power and resources. My spirit sinks to hear that the kings and rulers of Aryavart, the land of the great Aryans, have surrendered to the authority of the sultan.'

Then staring into space, she added, 'This attitude of throwing up your hands will lead you nowhere. Unless you resolutely decide to fight against this injustice, this atrocity and unprovoked attack on your territory, nothing is possible.'

Padmini's forceful assertion rendered Veerbhan speechless. However, he decided to continue to dominate the conversation, whichever way he could. 'I do respect your noble sentiments, Ranisa, but sometimes we need to understand the ground reality and the reality is . . .'

Padmini cut him short. 'A king worth his salt would not be the victim of circumstances, which you call reality.

Rather, he creates and conditions it. He makes his own destiny. He is duty-bound to protect the poor and helpless. If he himself dithers, what will be the fate of his subjects? In that case, they will be exposed to unchecked injustice, humiliation and unethical practices. There will be no place for avowed principles, high ideals and values. History is replete with examples where even the greatest and most affluent kings, who lived in luxury and completely neglected their citizens, have vanished from the face of the earth because they could not muster up the courage to wage a war against their opponents. It is adharma to bow your head before a demon out to invade your freedom and dignity. If you abandon dharma, no god will come to your rescue. It is extremely deplorable if the common citizens feel insecure. Let us for a moment consider that we will be defeated, but even in that eventuality, our self-respect will win. And as long as we are able to protect our self-respect, the name of our state will remain indelible in the annals of history.'

Veerbhan was stunned. Padmini's words carried the strength of her conviction. They did not grow in a vacuum. He did not have the courage to argue any further. A line of demarcation stood between his indifference towards Padmini and his disillusionment. Many and varied questions began to sprout within him. These were the questions, the importance of which lay in the fact that they arose even though they remained unanswered.

The swagger with which he had walked in began to recede. Padmini could sense it. She knew that in his heart of hearts, he was easy and sensitive and in search of answers.

Padmini reiterated, 'This proposal is shameful for Kshatriyas. Even a small ant would not desist from biting, as fiercely as possible, when trampled upon. What about you? You are going to be the king of this land, my son!'

The word 'son' slipped out of her mouth of its own. But the moment she said it, some remote corner of her heart throbbed for a moment.

'Do not underestimate the common people of this state. The sentiments of bravery, valour and sacrifice are deeply and permanently embedded in them. In fact, these are the virtues they hold high. Here, within everybody, there is something that is bigger than them. Within you, too, there is someone greater. I want you to listen to that somebody, that inner person. The initiation of a prince begins on the very day of his coronation. The first thing he ought to know is that a king with strong determination and loyal subjects makes for a worthy state.'

Veerbhan was trying, unsuccessfully, to stay poised. Padmini had not only hurt him but also managed to provoke him to think anew. He was finding it difficult to be indifferent.

Softening her tone, Padmini added, 'This fort is not merely a structure of bricks and stone. It is the embodiment of our self-respect. In order to protect this self-respect, umpteen numbers of patriots have laid down their lives valiantly. Lineages of various faiths, the Vedics, the Shaivas, the Jains, the Buddhists, have made this land sacred. You should not forget its glorious tradition and your past with all its achievements. Do not, for heaven's sake, desecrate them by handing over the respected daughter-in-law of this family to that licentious rogue.'

Veerbhan didn't argue. He silently regarded this queen before him who had managed to invoke his love and pride for Mewar, his motherland, with her assertive words. Why didn't anyone in the presiding committee remember this pride? A conflict was brewing within him, pulling him in two diametrically opposite directions. A strangely grave expression spread over his countenance as though he was fighting a war within. He stood there quietly, lost in himself.

He dropped his eyes and fixed them on the ground. The inner conflict began to show on his face. Placed in a dilemma over whether to agree with Padmini or not, his mind continuously encircled an indefinable orbit.

He remained there for some time. Then abruptly, without saying anything, he bowed low to Padmini. Still unable to meet her eyes, and still deep in thought, he turned around and left.

After Veerbhan had left, an uneasy silence reigned in the palace. Padmini didn't realize how shaken she was until the prince left. She played and replayed her conversation with Veerbhan in her head. *Where had the words come from?* She wondered what his actions would be. She knew her conviction had moved something in him. Yet, she dared not hope for any positive outcome. The mixed feelings of desperation, indignation and disgrace reflected on her face.

A storm of conflicting thoughts was raging inside her; her mind oscillated ceaselessly from hope to despair. A glimmer of hope now had been overtaken by a dampening apprehension within moments.

No positive thought—not even one—could stay in her mind for long. But why was it that the tendrils of hope refused to break? There was *something* in the depths of her heart, but what was it? She could not bring herself to ascertain whether that something really existed or if it was just an illusion.

In anxiety, she wiped her face now and again.

What should I do? Should I leave myself at the mercy of Veerbhan?

She stood up and paced the room.

No, I can't do that.

Should I immolate myself?

No!

Should I compromise with the situation?

Every time these questions arose, her mind responded with a forceful 'No, no.' Her voice had turned into a thousand voices reverberating all around.

What should I do then? The question rang through her mind over and over again. After all, her existence depended on the answer to this question. Yet, she was unable to arrive at a decision. The storm in her mind continued unabated.

She felt as though she was standing alone at one end of the earth, with strong winds blowing away the sand from the desert, and she was unable to find her way.

Was she so weak that she would be blown away by circumstances like a twig? Was there no way other than abject surrender? Again, a voice rose from the bottomless depths of her inner-self: No! No! No!

What the advisory council had decided was immoral and a brazen assault on the virtues of truth and honour. I cannot accept it, she thought. Not that she was gratuitously adamant. She wanted the glorious traditions of the royal family to be preserved and protected at all costs. And this needed strong resolve and the strength of self-confidence.

I will revolt, she thought to herself.

But how and in what way? That was still unclear. It seemed as if everything was covered by a thick pall of the dust carried by strong winds, and all around there was dense fog. She was conscious of the fact that in moments of crisis, emotions need to be restrained. She was aware that it was only with patience and a balanced state of mind that one could arrive at right decisions. If she could not free herself from the clutches of indecisiveness at this moment, she thought to herself, she would be destroyed.

She lay down tired, heavy-eyed. Her own hand on her chest felt unbearably heavy. She didn't know when she fell asleep. Frightening dreams . . . a horribly fiendish woman . . . hell . . . a nether world strewn with human bodies and dollops of flesh . . . screams . . . moans of pain . . . loud guffaws . . . nauseating sex in the open . . . men and women being whipped, tortured, persecuted brazenly . . .

She woke up with a suppressed cry. Drenched in perspiration, she groped around in the dark recesses of her head. It seemed as if hordes of venomous serpents were slithering across her mind. *How do I bear this? How do I consent to the pain of being disgraced by the brazenness of an undeserved punishment?* She sat there for a long time staring into space as if looking at her ignoble, hideous future with open eyes. She let out a stifled cry, 'Unbearable!'

Padmini suddenly felt angry with everything that women had to go through: unjust customs, family traditions and the presence of dynastic honour. A cascade of memories came flooding back.

Mother had been especially fond of her. She doted on her. When she came out of the wedding pavilion after the ceremony was over, her mother, with all the affection in her voice, had wished that Padmini be blessed with a son. Father had wished her good luck at the time of departure and said lovingly, 'May you be blessed with all the comforts in your husband's place!' He added a word of advice, 'You have to uphold the prestige of your father's family with your exemplary conduct and behaviour there. Always remember that you are not only Maharawal Ratan Singh's wife, but also the mother of the future offspring of that family. You have to shoulder the serious responsibility of upholding and maintaining the honour and sacred traditions of that great dynasty. Your duties should be uppermost in your mind.'

The gravity of their blessings and the freshness of the memory brought tears to her eyes. The expression on Mother's face when she was bidding her adieu was deeply etched in her mind. Mother was gazing unblinkingly at Ratan Singh, the bridegroom. There was a lot of love and affection in her eyes for him, but the separation of her daughter had saddened her greatly. There was nameless apprehension, but the moment her eyes turned to Ratan Singh that feeling would dissipate. In that look, there was a combined feeling of faith and trust for Ratan Singh.

Padmini was about to board the chariot, when her father became emotional. Choked with affection, he said, 'May the All Merciful bestow His grace on you!'

Where is your All Merciful, Father? Tell me, where is He? Her heart cried with helplessness.

It was a moonless night. Everything was deathly still: the wind seemed to have dropped to nothingness; the copses stood silent like witnesses to a grief-stricken atmosphere. *Is it possible that all the planets and other celestial bodies have chosen to pause on the axis of that moment?* An endless expanse of darkness had spread. Padmini felt alone; like the only living creature awake; self-absorbed, burning silently like the undiminished orb of a lamp in the midst of impenetrable darkness. There was something unidentifiable inside her that wanted to jump out with vengeance. What was it that was moving about her mind unstoppably? She tried to shake the feeling off her. *What are you doing*, she admonished herself. She had very little time at her disposal; and she had to make the final decision of her life.

She brushed the tears away and stood up decisively. She had the right to choose her own way, she thought to herself. Nobody could take that away from her. She *had* to act courageously.

The courage of her convictions awakened something in her. How long could she suffer with patience? How long did she have to wait for *them* to be active, for someone to protect her? How long was she expected to sit quiet without taking any initiative? How long? Her inner strength rose. She was bristling with anger and excitement against her own helplessness. Her loyalty and sincerity, her wedding vows, her family values would never allow her to accept the proposal.

Suddenly, she felt an upsurge of immense strength and confidence.

No more delays. Any more delay will be dangerous. Life is a hard truth and should not be subjected to emotions of any kind. She knew that any action in this regard had to be taken extremely carefully, after considering all aspects seriously and not on the spur of the moment. It would be sheer foolishness to squander such hard-earned self-strength with a wrong move.

What is to be done then?
Whom to look to for support?
Whom to take into confidence?

There were questions and only questions. Her awakened consciousness was beset with unanswered questions.

She was mentally prepared to undergo any amount of suffering for the sake of her family honour and her duty as a virtuous wife. She could sacrifice her all, even her life. But she did not know how. Thoughts, one after another, crossed her mind.

Tired of thinking about it, her mind stopped working.

Whatever it is, something must be done. Thinking idly and doing nothing will not lead anywhere. I have to live; however painful this life might prove to be. If others are not doing anything, I will have to do something. It's time to act.

She sat on a chair near her bedstead. The night was passing and she was desperately searching for a path through the overgrown thorny bushes that had lacerated both her body and mind.

From somewhere faraway, a half-awake bird cried.

She was absorbed in her thoughts: how could one free the Rajan from the captivity of the invincible army of the mlechhas, the barbarians? Who would be brave enough to take up the cudgel head-on? The problem was she didn't know many people personally who could be trusted to handle the situation with wisdom, strategy and bravery.

The thought of Mahamantri Mahan Singh came to her mind instantly. *He is an expert in warfare and a seasoned*

adviser. Shall I go to him and request him to . . . ? But . . .
She arrested her thoughts.

He may not be the most suitable person for the task ahead. He is undoubtedly a great warrior. There is no dearth of physical and mental strength in him; I know that for certain. But perhaps, strategically, the quickness of his mind may not measure up to the need of the hour. The strategy that he would perhaps formulate may fall short of the desired finesse.

Next?

Ajay Singh of Sisod? She had met him already. She had great respect for him. He was a decent and dignified man who was very popular among the people. He, along with his elder brother Arsingh, had fought against the Turks in the battle of Malwa, which claimed the life of valiant Arsingh and left Ajay Singh seriously injured. He had to undergo prolonged treatment in Sisod. She had been told that he was much better now, but had not completely recovered.

Then who else it could be?

She thought of Badal, a brave young man. She had heard a lot about his courage. People were all praise for his good sense and judgement. She knew that he was at present holding the charge of defending important checkposts on the Dhori highway of the Mewar–Gujarat region and also the entryways on the inaccessible terrain of the Aravalis. A well-built man, he had the reputation of being powerful and brave with some experience in tactical warfare. The only hitch was that he was all of twenty or twenty-one years of age. Would it be advisable to assign him the charge of the mighty task of leading the operation, she wondered. Courage and zeal alone would not do. A well thought-out plan was equally, if not more, important. What if, in his zeal to accomplish the task fast, he made an error of judgement and fell into a trap?

What could the alternative be?

She couldn't think of any other options. She hardly knew anybody she could depend on. When you are living in comfort, you don't think you would need people to rescue you. It is only when you are in trouble that you need them.

This land has many brave men.

She was looking for a person who was held in high esteem for his personal power and dedication; one who commanded respect and would strike fear in the minds of others.

Suddenly the thought of Gora Rawat of the Chauhan dynasty came to her mind. *Why didn't I think of him before!*

She knew the influence he had on people at large. He had proved his worth on several occasions. He was a reserved and introspective person, not given to sharing much about himself.

She began to deliberate on this idea.

Even in the toughest of times he follows his dharma religiously.

Those who follow their dharma or discharge their duties honestly realize the truth automatically, she knew.

He had already fought the deadliest of wars displaying exemplary organizing capacity and valour. He had acquired complete expertise in strategic planning, military operation and growth of military power. He was fully equipped with the qualities required to lead operations: firmness, organizing capacity, ability to mobilize the forces, setting and achieving goals and targets. He had all those qualities based on which she could assign this responsibility to him. She remembered now how the Rajan had once said that Gora could be compared with the best warriors in the world. He had the ability to turn an adverse situation to an advantageous one when the situation demanded it. She had heard that he was a strong-willed person who was not swept away by emotions. And that he had the capability of finding the truth.

But what about the fear of what the king had ordained?

Likhvanbai once told her that Ala-ud-Din Khilji had planned to invade Gujarat around Samvat 1356 (1299 CE). He had to pass through the Dhori roads of Mewar because that was the only accessible link to Gujarat in those days. The entire region was under Gora's charge, who did not allow the Turks to go past. An armed confrontation had ensued between Ala-ud-Din's royal army and Gora's forces. The Turks were defeated. But, by that time, Maharawal Samar Singh, Ratan Singh's father, had judged the immensity of the power of Ala-ud-Din's army. Deciding not to get involved in the tussle, he allowed them to pass through their territory. Gora did not agree with the decision. Maharawal Samar Singh understood and respected his sentiments but was bound by his limitations. He did not want to invite trouble unnecessarily.

It was because of Raghav Chetan's chicanery that Gora was living on the sidelines. Raghav had poisoned Mahawaral Ratan Singh's mind against Gora. Influenced by him, the maharawal had suspended Gora.

It was Gora Rawat who had forbidden Raghav from entering the women's apartments without permission. His experienced eyes had sensed that Raghav was not only an evil soul but also a man of malicious intentions. Dedicating two hours to the practice of yoga early in the morning seemed to have made him believe that he was entitled to do anything.

Instigated by Raghav, the Rajan had punished the honest and dedicated Gora.

For a moment, Padmini felt anger flickering towards the Rajan. *Why was he pleased with dishonest hangers-on? Why did he treat honest, straightforward and plain-spoken persons as enemies? If, in this critical situation, Gora takes up the gauntlet, the people of this land will welcome it. All high-ranking officers of the state have great regard for him. Even Prince Veerbhan, as they say, is a great admirer of Gora.*

She stopped at the thought of Veerbhan. She seemed to have guessed that after their conversation, Veerbhan would have been in a state of inner conflict, with serious misgivings in his mind about the parishad's decision.

It is quite possible that he is going through a phase of indecisiveness. Now that he is struggling with indecision and doubts, it is the right time to approach him. His consent is most important at this juncture. Even now, it is not too late. I noticed that though he is not kindly disposed to me, he is not cruel at heart.

But she was not sure whether Gora Rawat would pay heed to any request; whether he would take the risk of making a commitment, and whether he could forget the insults heaped on him. She had her doubts. The Rajan had disregarded him, which he didn't deserve, and had denied him the credit he deserved.

What if one gets the cold shoulder on approaching him? And would the Rajan accept it calmly once he comes to know? Above all, would it be right to contact a suspended general?

The idea that she had enthused over took no time to dissipate. Various thoughts in conflict with each other took over. And again, in no time, she was in the grip of a dilemma. Once again, despair took over. Everything appeared to be in a state of utter confusion.

She regained her composure. *No, this apprehension is born out of the deep-seated fear in my heart during this hour of crisis.* She had to act not only as a faithful wife but as a queen. This was the moment of truth, the words flashed in her mind. She alone was the master of this moment.

How can subjecting a woman to indignity be an act of dharma? Righteousness is the spirit of dharma, which inspires one to act nobly and set ideals worth emulating. It opens up doors to a new liberation. The path of liberation does not follow a particular route. It has to be discovered.

Gora was a brave man. Bravery was deeply embedded in his character. Besides, he was a man of wisdom who would pull out all the stops to protect the truth. He had to be approached. There was no other option.

It would be her first and last effort.

The more she thought about it, the stronger her resolve became and the faster her ambivalence dissolved.

This decision cannot be delayed further; it cannot be put off till tomorrow because tomorrow exists only in the realm of imagination. It never comes. What exists in reality is today; this very moment. It's now or never. I must go.

As soon as this thought took root in her mind, she decided to act on it. She got up and felt as though the power of every nerve, of every fibre, had converged; her past life and all that the future held had merged into the present. Drawing strength from an unknown source of inspiration, she was filled with tremendous self-assertion. There was no ambiguity, no conflict and no uncertainty in her mind.

'I must go and meet him.'

Deep in her heart she felt a feeble ruddy glow akin to the first light that appears at dawn to dispel the darkness of the night.

An unflagging steadiness was growing in her heart. It was an unfamiliar, incorporeal strength. Breaking away from her image as a soft and delicate person, she girded herself to face the situation with determination and courage. She believed that noble thoughts and sacred affirmations had the blessings of God. With this thought in mind, she felt as if a weight had been lifted off her. The silent powers of nature seemed to give her strength. She had a feeling that some unknown forces were taking care of her.

The night was nearing its end. Some stars were still twinkling. The dim light of early dawn had started spreading.

Sugna stayed awake till late. Padmini was conscious of her presence all through. Sitting close to the door constantly, Sugna had dozed off and slumped to the floor. Padmini shook her gently to wake her. 'Sugna! Sugna!'

Sugna woke up with a start and squinted. Before she was fully awake, Padmini said to her, 'Sugna! Go and get the palanquin ready. I have to go right now, at this very moment.'

Bewildered, she stared at Padmini quizzically. Half asleep, half awake, she couldn't understand what the matter was. Her eyebrows narrowed. It was not very often that Rani Padmini went out of her apartment. When she did, it was to go to the temple or to attend some special celebration. *But why today? And all of a sudden? That too at this odd hour?* She stared at her Ranisa open-mouthed. At that moment, Padmini did not look like her usual self: simple and innocent as a child. Sugna was confused. Unable to think clearly, she kept sitting apprehensively.

'Hurry up before anybody asks why and wherefore,' Padmini said, 'There's no time to answer any questions. Be quick and call the attendants. Ask them to spruce up the palanquin.'

Sugna rearranged her apparel and was about to leave when Padmini impressed upon her the gravity of the situation. 'Tell the attendants that they have to take Ranisa to Gora Rawat's residence. Tell them to be ready immediately as they have to set off early, before the sun rises.'

Just as Sugna mechanically turned to go out, Padmini cautioned her, 'Don't let anybody else know. Just get the palanquin ready and come back.'

* * *

Made of sandalwood, the palanquin was adorned with strings of pearls and gems. Padmini, accompanied by Sugna, sat inside. A new sense of optimism was pervading her in an atmosphere where people were gripped by a sense of impending gloom. She looked out from the curtained window. Not a soul was in sight. The streets were deserted. Every home, every doorpost, every door and every panel appeared to bow down silently in despair.

But Padmini was seeing far beyond; she had retreated into her world of thoughts. For a brief moment, a question arose in her mind. Did she take the decision of discussing the matter with Gora all of a sudden, or was the idea already embedded in her mind?

The palanquin moved at a steady pace. Its rhythm slowly calmed the turmoil in her mind. The wind was light and the weather seemed quite favourable.

The palanquin was close to Gora's house. She looked out and saw that somebody, not clearly identifiable, was standing on one side of the house. She looked at the figure carefully and felt that it might be Gora himself. Standing outside what looked like a stable, a man was stroking a white horse fondly. The steed had turned its neck backwards and was swishing its tail and neighing.

The man did not miss the palanquin heading in his direction. Startled, he tried to scrutinize it. It seemed to be the royal palanquin from the queen's apartment. There was no mistake; it was definitely coming towards his residence. He became alert and began to watch carefully.

Sugna emerged from the palanquin and asked the bearers, 'Is this the house of Gora Rawat? Are you sure?'

'Gora Rawat's house is a well-known place in Chittor,' replied the youngest attendant.

The morning light had not spread completely. In the dim light, Gora could not see or understand anything clearly. However, from the concern in the voice of the woman standing at a distance, he guessed there was certainly something serious and confidential. He pulled the bridle, turned the horse to one side and positioned it well out of harm's way. Then he approached them and said, 'Yes, I am Gora. Why did you take the trouble to come to this humble servant's residence?'

Sugna bowed respectfully and said, 'Maharani Padmini has come to seek your advice. She wants to consult you.'

'Rani Padmini?' Gora was stunned. For a moment he couldn't believe his ears. Before he could say anything, Padmini stepped out of the royal palanquin. Gora bowed and paid obeisance to her. Most humbly, he said, 'Why did you take the trouble, Ranisa? You should have sent for me, your servant, instead.'

Padmini looked admiringly at Gora's slim and well-built body. His strong frame reminded her of Sage Dadhichi. Stories suggested that the sage had offered his bones to the gods for them to make a thunderbolt, which Indra used to defeat Vritasur and other demons. Strength radiated from his body, and on his face was the glow of a mighty warrior. There was no look of acrimony or resignation on his face. Though he was gentle, absolutely dignified with affection in his eyes and serenity on his face, adversity had made him intense and earnest.

With utmost respect, he ushered the younger queen of Mewar into his house. Devoid of all trappings of luxury and comfort, the room was almost bare. On one side, a white sheet, clean but very old, had been spread on the floor. In one corner, on a small table, was a sharp arrow attached to a bowstring.

It didn't take her long to understand that Gora had sold all his belongings to save his self-respect.

He said deferentially, 'The women and children of the house have gone to the temple of Samidheshwar. A night-long vigil of devotional singing has been organized there. I was with them and had just returned. With your permission, may I go and bring them back to welcome you?'

'No, no. Let them enjoy themselves. This is no time for formality. I have come here for a special purpose.'

Gora couldn't fathom what the queen wanted to say. Curiously, he said, 'Please give me a command, Ranisa!'

'You know what has happened and how it happened. Now that we are facing a bad time, you should forget and forgive everything. I beg of you. I have come to you with a lot of hope and trust. And this trust is not without reason,' replied Padmini.

'Please don't embarrass me. It'll be my privilege to obey your orders, Ranisa! It will be my good fortune to be able to prove my loyalty.' His self-consciousness did not go away completely, but he started speaking more freely.

Padmini watched Gora closely, carefully. Despite doubts lingering in her mind, she wanted to be sure if he was genuinely committing himself or if he was saying so just to give her false hopes. She felt a huge surge of relief and happiness to see a glint of determination in his eyes. She wanted to make it clear, in no uncertain terms, that she always had full faith in him and that she firmly believed that he would be able to protect the honour of Mewar.

She narrated to him in detail the incident of Veerbhan's visit and the parishad's decision that was conveyed to her. Coming straight from her heart, each and every word was drenched in pain. Recalling the conversation, she felt as though her entire being was smouldering. Every now and again, her throat would constrict, bringing tears to her eyes.

Gora heard her till the end with unwavering concentration. Her otherwise composed visage quivered a little every now and then. Even though he was listening to her intently, a whole stream of thoughts ran alongside in his head.

After she had finished, the queen said, 'I have come here to remind you of your capabilities. The whole of Chittor knows that you are brave, a veteran warrior full of energy and vigour, and above all, you have always taken a righteous and principled stand.'

Gora didn't say a word. Lost in labyrinthine thoughts, he was silent and grim-faced. Padmini gazed at him with unblinking eyes. He was her last hope. She felt that his heart, too, was as heavy as her own. Padmini said piteously, 'The life of the Rajan, as well as my honour, is at stake. I have come to you with the hope that you will protect us.'

'Please don't embarrass me again and again, Ranisa! I am fully conscious of my responsibilities during this difficult time. I do not know how far I'll be able to succeed in my efforts, but I'd stop at nothing to do all I can and should do.' His eyes were moist with intense emotions; his voice revealed a firm assurance.

Deep in thought again, he had absolutely no doubt about what his mission entailed. It was only the nuances of how he would go about fulfilling it that needed to be drawn out.

Adverse conditions had made Gora very patient. There was no trace of worry or distress lining his face. When he emerged from his train of thoughts, he said, 'You need not worry, Ranisa. I assure you, he will never succeed in his sinful design.' His humble yet assertive tone came straight from the core of his heart. The assurance in Gora's words strengthened her confidence that he would be able to rise to the challenge.

Padmini wanted to tread cautiously, which is why she wanted Gora to seek consent from Prince Veerbhan, to whom the king would pass on the baton. 'Prince Veerbhan's consent is necessary. So, before finalizing any plan, we must have his permission. The responsibility of bringing him around has to be shouldered by you.'

Seeing the pain deepening in her eyes, Gora said reassuringly, 'Don't worry about that, please. I know him personally. I know his character well. The enthusiasm to do something, and also some impatience, are part of his personality. He is gentle and easy to be with, which is why he is unable to hide his emotions. It will not be difficult for us to explain to him that justice and morality demand that we fight for our self-respect. When he visited you, he must have been under some momentary pressure. This is not his inherent nature. But rest assured, this servant of yours will not finalize any plan without his consent.'

Despite this, the apprehensions in Padmini's mind were not completely resolved. She said, 'Before formulating any plan of action, we need to consider all aspects of the matter.

The terror in our minds, a sense of gloom and failure, and a defeatist attitude has made this task even more difficult. I have unshakable faith in you, which prompted me to approach you. But we need the support and involvement of other military generals and warlords as well. They, too, have to be taken into confidence. When fear intensifies, it takes time to awaken courage in people. We have to make them realize their inner strength and self-confidence in a very short time. The brazenness and ferocity of the tyrant has weakened their morale and fighting spirit. It is, therefore, incumbent on you to awaken in them the dormant Kshatriya dharma, the heroism of a born warrior.'

A gentle radiance came over Gora's face.

Padmini continued, 'The people are despondent. Fear of death has gripped them. This does not augur well for our state. We need to attack this frustrated mindset and help them regain courage and confidence.'

'I understand what you expect from me, Ranisa! Your humble servant will proceed according to your wishes.'

Padmini's mind was crowded with all kinds of thoughts. But she was not as perturbed as before. Gora's support had pacified her.

After a pause, Gora said, 'Ranisa, I too have a request to make.'

'Please go ahead,' Padmini raised her head to look at him.

'My elder brother, Gavan, has a son. His name is Badal.'

'Yes, I have heard of him.'

'He is a brave and sharp-minded warrior. He is not merely a skilled fighter; he has something deeper inside him. He confronted the Turks when he was posted at the Lion Gate, through which the paths from the Narmada valley on the north head towards the south. From the garrison atop the hillside, he foiled the royal forces' attempts at intruding into our territory. He made the blockade impenetrable for the Turks. I feel that he may prove to be a pillar of great strength in this fight. If you personally ask him to join me in our operation, he will do so with added enthusiasm.'

An expression of reassuring confidence returned to his eyes.

'Indeed. I too am curious about his acts of bravery and remarkable capabilities. Where can I meet him?'

'He should be here any moment. Every morning he goes to a big playground to hone his horsemanship as part of his daily exercise.'

Just then they heard a horse outside. Gora went out of the room.

Padmini began to wonder how the brave Gora had agreed to face the enemy without any fear or second thought. His lack of hesitation indicated clarity of thought, as though any inner conflict, lack of fearlessness, and aimlessness were not part of his nature. It was apparent that he did not have to think twice. He had suffered so much, and yet he had indomitable faith in life.

Gora returned with Badal. Padmini looked at him, a twenty-or twenty-two-year-old strapping, young lad. Regular exercise and vigorous tasks had ensured his body was well-sculpted, sinewy and powerful. A fire-like glow shone on his face, and his personality as a whole had an unusual agility, discipline, sturdiness, enthusiasm and a spirit of dedication.

Badal bowed to her in deference.

'Is there anything I can do for you, Ranisa?'

'Badal! I have come here to put you in danger.'

'What danger? A Rajput is born to play with danger,' said Badal evenly.

'I have heard a lot about your determination, your admirable fighting skills and your being a man of great insight. Keeping in view these qualities, I am assigning you a task. You have to rescue the maharawal from the clutches of the sultan of Delhi. You have to protect the honour of Padmini by any means.'

If he could stand any straighter, Badal would have. His face seemed to glow at the sound of her words. Almost as if impatient to fight the enemy right away, he said, 'I will mobilize hundreds of brave warriors to fight for this cause and see that the earth is covered with the corpses of the enemy forces.'

Padmini signalled him to stop and said, 'First, listen to what I say and then give me your opinion.' He stood still. She continued in a solemn tone, 'I am sorry to say that despite Gora's admirable qualities, the maharawal is not favourably disposed towards him these days. I don't know how he would respond to the proposal of him leading the campaign. Perhaps he would not give Gora the honour he deserves. So, you have to do it not only as your duty as a devoted soldier, but also with a humanitarian approach, without expecting anything in return. Selflessly.'

Gora stood without saying a word. But Badal was as blistering as the summer sun. 'Uncle Gora considers a task done with a selfish motive not only improper but an act of adharma,' he said. 'Even otherwise, principles are greater than any individual.'

Padmini looked at the young man in front of her. Badal appeared to be brimming with courage and vigour, with no trace of fear and apprehension. 'It does not behove the brave to give up efforts for fear of unfavourable results. Ranisa, if you have any other apprehensions, please tell us. We will give you our word only after that.'

'Yes, I do,' said Padmini, 'I have yet another apprehension that is troubling me. How will your wives react? They will certainly curse me for putting the lives of their husbands at stake for the sake of my own honour and my husband's life.'

For the first time, Gora's face betrayed some emotion. With flaring nostrils, he said, 'No, no, Ranisa! Do not let this thought enter your mind. The wives of Kshatriyas do not shed tears over the heroic death of their husbands. On the contrary, they prepare their men to go to the battlefield by handing them weapons. Moreover, a king is the master of the state. Please do not compare this lowly, humble, insignificant person to our revered king.'

Badal's fierceness became more pronounced. He went to a corner and picked up the shining arrow lying on the table. He pricked his arm with its sharp point. Out came a tiny stream of blood with which he smeared the palm of his hand and went over to Padmini. 'Ranisa, I swear by this blood! Maharawal Ratan Singh will be back on the throne and the honour of Rani Padmini will stand protected even if a number of brave soldiers have to sacrifice their lives.' His eyes flashed as he said this. He put the arrow back on the table and wiped the blood trickling from his arm with a sweep of his hand. A few drops of blood still glistened on the head of the arrow.

Padmini looked at Badal admiringly. Enamoured with his words, his show of courage and unflinching loyalty, she was wondered if there were others around who would stand before his brilliance.

'You are the bravest of the brave in the true sense, Badal! You deserve special praise. I feel that my hope has been strengthened. May Lord Eklingji bestow his grace on you so as to enable you to remain steadfast in your pledge.'

Badal offered a cheerful smile.

Padmini rose from her seat and said, 'I am thankful to you both.'

'You need not thank us. In fact, we feel honoured by your visit. We are grateful that you reposed trust in us and made us realize our duty towards the state, thus, giving us a purpose to live.'

Padmini was about to leave when her worries returned. Gora was quick to read the queen's mind. In a consolatory tone, he said, 'Don't you worry, Ranisa! We assure you that we will obey your order in letter and spirit. To us, your word is more sacrosanct than our scriptures.'

Padmini felt their assuring words resounding around her, as though they had come from some other world. She felt invigorated.

'We are fortunate that you came and purified our humble abode with the dust of your feet,' Gora said deferentially.

Gora and Badal bowed to her. For a moment, she gazed admiringly at the embodiments of valour. Then she went and sat in the palanquin.

As the palanquin left for the palace, the despondency that had weighed her down seemed to have been lifted. They had sufficiently assured her with their support. She almost felt buoyant. Her perturbed mind was filled with a sense of solace. She took a deep breath, inhaling the cool morning air.

How resolute, and yet profound, is Gora! The adverse situations in his life have perhaps taught him to be patient and determined. He is so brave and yet so humble.

And Badal! There is unlimited courage flowing in his veins. How impatient he is, looking to take up the challenge in an instant. How full he was of hope, as though the freedom of the king from the enemy's custody was not simply a wish but the complete truth. It's amazing that such a strong personality has developed within him at this tender age. Badal is not only incomparable but also a role model; an example to be emulated by the young generation.

Gora is cool and sober, and Badal is just the opposite: aggressive with a fire in his belly. But they are so similar in their thinking and their philosophy of life. Worries or despondency have not touched them. It seems fear will never be able to pick up the courage to confront them. People say that Badal was raised under Gora's care and protection. Perhaps the similarity is because of this bond. They have a lot of self-confidence. One can trust only those who have confidence in themselves.

The palanquin continued to make its way towards the palace.

When Veerbhan had conveyed the parishad's message to her, she had felt as though everything around her had crashed: the pride of the family, the honour of womanhood, the safety of the king, their dignity. A thorn piercing all these layers had finally struck the most vulnerable part of her—'I'.

The 'I' of her ego, smouldering silently, had burst into a fire. How had her intelligence, her wisdom worked in that situation? Which was that moment that gave her tormented mind a dogged determination? What kind of introspection had led to this decision? At this moment, she was unable to understand it. Whatever the decision, she had made up her mind to take it, whether it was judged right or not; whether it was in the overall interest of Chittor or merely her own.

She heard another voice inside her head: 'The pride and honour of Chittor and your own honour as the king's wife are not different things. It is in the pride and dignity of Chittor that your honour lies. Is your existence separate from Chittor?'

What is this existence of mine? Until this day, she had been unable to realize what her presence meant. It was for the first time in the ultimate moments of this dense darkness that she had come face-to-face with her being. It was in these moments that her independent identity had come to the fore for the first time. After she had been carried away by the strong currents of agony, emotional deprivation and humiliation with nothing to hold on to, she could finally see herself in a definitive frame.

Overtaken by the night-long tiredness, she felt as though there was no energy left in her body. However, a new voice of hope emerged from within: 'Do not worry. Things will turn in your favour.'

A strange intoxication of faith and hope overtook her.

The curtains of the palanquin fluttered, ushering in the early morning cool breeze. When she peered through the rippling silk, she caught the glow of dawn on the eastern horizon.

The city was agog with excitement. The news that Gora had risen to the challenge spread like wildfire. He was to address a select gathering of soldiers, generals, nobles, vassals and warlords in the assembly hall.

A wave of elation ran through the terrified citizens. There was something to do; a heave on the surface that could mean something more than merely facing assault with their hands tied. And it was also because they had immense love and trust for Gora and Badal.

Once the stir began, the course of events started picking up pace. An atmosphere of expectancy prevailed.

The auditorium was packed with warriors of all ranks. People continued to stream in. It looked as though the number of people waiting outside outnumbered those inside the hall. Common people were not allowed to enter, but their curiosity to read the future course of action from the expressions of the generals was irrepressible.

Padmini occupied a seat close to the latticed gallery on the upper floor of the auditorium, from where she could watch the proceedings. Seated behind were her attendants and other women from her apartment.

Ajay Singh, Bhim Singh, Sangram Singh, Bagh Singh, Bhawani Singh, Jaitaran, Surya Mal and other distinguished personalities entered the jam-packed hall.

The courtiers rose. The tumult came to a halt.

The front row was occupied by the members of the war council. Soon after, Prince Veerbhan, followed by Mahamantri Mahan Singh and Gora and Badal, appeared. Once again, all the assembled members were on their feet and silence prevailed.

Padmini glanced at the members of the war council in the front row. Suddenly, she noticed a ten- to twelve-year-old boy among them. A unique mixture of innocence and solemnity was visible on his face. He had a strong physique and long arms, not normally seen among boys his age. He was observing the proceedings with rapt attention.

That good-looking boy with a seraphic grace took her breath away. Who was he? She signalled Sugna, who was sitting close by, to come to her. 'Is Likhvanbai here?' she asked.

'Yes, she is here. Shall I call her?'

'Please do.'

Likhvanbai was there in a moment. There was a courteous look on her face and a shine in her eyes. Age had not dented her agility and vigour. The reddish glow on her copper face reflected her knowledge and wisdom.

'Is there anything I can do for you, Ranisa?'

'Bai!' said Padmini, 'Who is that boy sitting in the front row?'

Likhvanbai fixed her gaze at the boy, trying to recognize him. 'You mean the one seated next to Ajay Singh?'

'Yes, that boy.'

'He is the son of late Ara Singh, the eldest son of Lakshman Singh, who was a brave fighter of the Mandalik fort in Sisod. His name is Hamir. He is the heir to the *jagir*, the estate of Sisod.'

'Hamir's father was killed in the battle of Malwa recently. After Ara Singh's heroic death, his wife performed jauhar by jumping into the fire to save her honour,' she continued.

'Under whose care and protection is he being brought up, Bai?'

'Ajay Singh, his father's younger brother, is his guardian. Ajay Singh himself was seriously injured in the battle of Malwa. He was under treatment for a long time in Sisod. After his recovery, it is for the first time that he has participated in the state's activities.'

Lakshman Singh was a brave warrior and a skilled strategist. But he was away in Malwa. He had twelve sons, all of whom were brave like their father. He was the most powerful person in Mewar, next only to the maharawal, the king. He held an influential position in the state. The king had great respect for him and considered him his elder brother.

Likhvanbai told Padmini that in Mewar, the first ruler of the Guhil dynasty was King Bapa Rawal. He ruled the state for a long time and then chose to take *sanyaas* and renounce the throne. After him, many brave and courageous rulers of the dynasty ascended the throne. During the reign of Raja Karna, the Guhil dynasty branched into two dynasties named after his sons—Rawal and Rana.

The elder son, Rawal, became the king of Mewar. The younger one defeated a formidable enemy and earned the title of 'Rana'. He reclaimed the territory of Sisod and became its ruler. The Rana dynasty continued to rise in power and prominence. Lakshman Singh belonged to this dynasty. The royal set-up of Sisod was the most important principality in the area.

The hall was filled to capacity. Once the initial formalities were complete, Gora rose to address the assembly. All eyes were on him. He radiated confidence.

In his typical style of addressing a gathering of important people, he began to speak. The tone of his voice was cool, serious and deep. 'Friends, we are assembled here to give our thoughts to the current situation in all its perspective. We know that we are faced with grave and critical circumstances, and we have very little time at our disposal.' He paused for a moment before continuing, 'The brave and valorous would not shy away from fighting the enemy for fear of loss or defeat. We are the soldiers of the ruler whose ancestor, Bapa Rawal, had crushed the Turks who came from Sindh. Emperor Bisaldeo too had chased them out of the land of Aryavart. Maharawal Samar Singh had put the *Yavanas*, the Arab invaders, to rout. Why are we afraid of the enemy? Why are we thinking about handing over the queen of Mewar to the sultan? It will be very disgraceful and cowardly of us if we choose to avoid a battle in exchange for our Ranisa. Such an undignified surrender will prove to be far more deadly than the poison *halahal*. In this hour of crisis, when we are faced with grave challenges and threats, we must not forget that a soldier's field of action is the battlefront, where he has to fight and lay down his life in order to defend the country's honour and values.'

All the soldiers and other members of the war council listened to the man before them, weighing each and every word he spoke. Gora's deep voice, his wisdom and the strength of his character resonated with the audience before him. He analysed the impending situation in a matter-of-fact manner.

Taking a pause, he swept a glance over every member present there. What he had to say must capture their minds and convince them. He said earnestly, 'It is not a one-off problem. This has to be viewed in a broader perspective. It will be a great mistake on our part to think that the sultan will sit quiet once the queen is handed over to him. It is not for the first time that the Yavanas have attacked, nor is this going to be the last. By handing over our queen to him, do you think we will kill the crisis? Do you think the enemy will leave?'

He scanned the crowd again, looking for a response, commanding a response. Many shuffled their feet, many lowered their eyes. Gora continued, 'You can put off the crisis for now, but you cannot do so for all time to come. If you give in to a bully, it will only enhance his greed. Plundering and causing all-round destruction has caught the fancy of this power-drunk barbarian to the point of obsession. He thinks that he can establish his rule over any territory by running roughshod over its people.'

The audience was all ears, accepting Gora's words of wisdom as scriptural injunctions. It looked as though sparks were flying off Gora's eyes. The radiance of his personal vigour was spreading like sunlight. He stopped. He surveyed the gathering again. If eyes could speak eloquently then his eyes made more declarations than his words. All of them kept looking at him.

Padmini gazed at Gora with admiration. As his words echoed in the assembly hall, she felt calm, as if it was finally all right to breathe, to be. She felt that his words carried imperishable truth and undiminished strength. She was amazed to find that Gora had immediately established an emotional connect with his audience. Her heart was filled with respect for him.

You are a man in the truest sense—a rare coalescence of emotional intensity, persuasive argument and an aggressive sense of duty. In this hour of despair and despondency, you stand as firm as a rock.

Raising his voice, Gora said fiercely, 'The straight and shorter route to the Haj pilgrimage passes through Mewar. The pilgrims prefer the Gujarat coast for their journey towards Mecca and other shrines in Arabia. The port of Surat is the commercial hub of Aryavart or Bharat. Again, it is through Mewar that different places in northern, eastern, western and southern parts of the country can be reached. Our kingdom is situated at the centre and, therefore, it is the nerve centre of trade and commerce, besides being perfectly suited for military operations, with suitable infrastructure like better roads and highways. We are in a strong position to dismantle infrastructural support and ensure the roads leading to Malwa and Gujarat are unserviceable, if and when the situation demands.' The crowd murmured and stirred.

Gora paused. What he said next came out almost like a roar.

'The enemy can control a vast expanse of territory extending from Delhi to Malwa and the provinces of Gujarat so long as there is nobody to disrupt their movement. The sultan would want to ensure that these highways are safe for travelling. It is obvious that unless they are under his control, he cannot effectively exercise administrative control over Delhi, Malwa and Gujarat. Besides, Malwa is among the most powerful kingdoms and principalities in the country. So, unless the sultan conquers Chittor, he will not be able to exercise authority unhindered over the length and breadth of his empire.'

Padmini's eyes widened. Her heart beat faster realizing what Gora was saying. Her eyes scanned the crowd. What were they thinking?

The pitch of Gora's voice and the intensity of his emotional appeal continued to rise. His speech continued to flow like an uninterrupted river. Padmini looked at the assembly watching their hero wordlessly, unblinkingly.

The light of determination in Gora's eyes became more intense. The audience hung on to every word. Even his pauses seemed measured. They allowed the information he reeled out to be processed. Gora's eyes blazed, and the audience seemed buzzed with the power of his conviction. 'If all the kings and rulers of Aryavart go on submitting to this impious sultan one after another, the independence and sovereignty of all the states, their cultural identity, their traditional wisdom and thinking will come to an end. Friends, be brave. You must keep in mind that the sultan's rule and his forces are not going to last forever, whereas our dharma and this great land of ours will live for eternity.'

Padmini's gaze swept the assembly hall. The atmosphere was charged with an emotional upsurge. The true face of the tyrant and his nefarious designs had been exposed. The darkness of the caverns began to dispel, ushering in rays of light that rekindled hope. A sense of optimism began to surge in them, which dissipated their cowardice. It looked as though they had entered a woodland with an ambience of magical valour, where there would be faced with miseries and hardships, but fear and despair there was not.

Her eyes rested on that winsome boy again. His eyes were shining with a vague but intense curiosity. Indifferent to others around him, the boy looked as though he was lost in the world of Gora's thoughts. He stared at Gora with his mouth open. It was as if he was drinking in Gora's words. A new world of action and knowledge was opening up before him. Padmini could not take her eyes off the boy, Hamir, whose face was aglow like the rising sun.

A strange attraction seemed to pull her towards him. If only she had a child of her own like him, her life would be justified, she thought.

Suddenly, she was reminded of the tribal woman nursing her baby by the roadside en route to Chittor. The woman had gazed at her child with so much love and affection! At that moment, a sliver of a thought rose in her. It left her blushing.

If only she could be a mother. If only she could have the good luck of undergoing labour pain, of holding a baby in her arms, of nursing it, of watching the baby toddle and play . . . an old wound began to open. She wanted to believe that everything was finished, yet she had no control over her irrepressible hope.

The yearning that had bloomed inside her lingered on silently.

The force in Gora's voice continued to mount. Each and every word carried a spark of inspiration. His eyes blazed with passion. Prince Veerbhan listened to him gravely. Padmini, lost in her thoughts, remained cut-off from the world.

Gora's words loosened a torrent of patriotic sentiment. 'Friends and warriors, for thousands of years we have worshipped this land, undergone severe penance and performed yajnas, sacrificial rituals, and followed a strict regime of virtuous conduct for the sake of our motherland. Will you now allow this holy land to be spoiled by the devilish game of the enemy? Can you let our revered Ranisa surrender to them and sit quietly, unperturbed? Will you allow this demonic power to succeed in its nefarious designs for fear of defeat?' He shot his questions like arrows from his quiver.

'No! No!' A thousand voices resonated in unison. That formidable resonance seemed to carry a force strong enough to tear apart the impregnable walls of the enemy establishment and shake its foundation.

A frenzy of cries seeking retribution filled the air.

'Very well! Superb!' The veterans nodded in approval. The expression on the prince's face clearly showed that Gora had his support.

The eyes, which were carrying shadows of despair till a while ago, were now gleaming with a sense of pride and self-esteem. The assembly was thrilled.

'This wicked, power-hungry sultan does not deserve any courtesy, much less any gift. Friends, we cannot protect our dharma by meekly and disgracefully submitting to his immoral demands. It is by laying down our lives that we can protect and preserve it. You have to be prepared to give up your life for the sake of dharma, the sacred principles, and the truth.'

Gora rallied his troops and generals, breathing new life into their fading spirits. His words acted like magical preachments. Patriotic sentiments began to swell in them. The fighting spirit, the courage that they had lost, had never left them. It was as if a veil had been lifted. All their dormant potentialities had been awakened. They felt as though nothing was impossible. Their pessimistic thoughts disappeared and they were fired-up with enthusiasm. Gora had struck the right notes that produced muted chants of 'Arise! Awake!' in their hearts. A single lamp had lit a string of lamps. Everybody got up and shouted to demonstrate their solidarity with Gora's appeal. The rising tide of their voices created a deafening tumult.

The gravitas in Gora's voice and posture remained unchanged. He observed the response from the gathering. With tremendous confidence in his eyes he raised his hands, gesturing the crowd to calm down. They obeyed him.

'We have to fight but not with a self-sacrificial mindset. A determined fighting force is complete in itself even without adequate financial resources and military strength. The first and foremost principle of fighting a battle is the skill; an unwavering desire to trounce the enemy. A battle begins with the resolve to win it. Those who accept defeat even before going to the battlefield can never challenge the enemy decisively.'

How powerful and motivating his words are!

A wave of a strong, yet pious, desire to stand and act spread through the crowd. Their battered morale began to get a much-needed boost. The determination to face the crisis courageously and come out victorious became stronger.

'We have to face the invaders with complete unity. We know what our areas of vulnerability are. But if we have the vision to see our goal and the courage to achieve it, we can defeat the enemy.'

The conch shell was sounded to signal that the meeting was over. People began to troop out with a strong resolve to win.

Padmini watched the people leave in high spirits. She couldn't help but say admiringly, 'Gora! You are great! This campaign needs your leadership.'

Meanwhile, the members of the war council, some distinguished soldiers and nobles went into a huddle in the conference room. They were engaged in finalizing the operational and strategic roadmap. Their secret discussion continued late into the night.

***

Dawn broke with a strange excitement in the air. The atmosphere was charged with a nameless, soundless enthusiasm. There was a hush in the air as people dared not breathe a word. The frenetic activity of armed soldiers had turned the area into a garrison town. Messengers were doing the rounds of the city frantically, busy delivering secret messages to the authorities, who in turn were issuing instructions and orders to be followed by commanders and others. Every movement, every activity was cloaked in a shroud of mystery. It was difficult to read the minds of the people from their expressions. Everyone wore a mask of seriousness, but the spark in their eyes gave away the excitement. The sentries, as well as the mounted cavalrymen, were guarded, as if anticipating some unexpected development.

People in this land approached both life and death in the most dignified manner. When in a celebratory mood, they enjoyed life to the fullest. Yet when it came to facing adversity, they held themselves with extreme restraint. Sugna came back with hair oil and a comb. She spoke to Padmini solicitously, 'Shall I call Lakshmi? She'll tidy your hair. You have not loosened it in three days. You need a good comb.'

'I don't feel like it now,' said Padmini half-consciously.

How could she be particular about her appearance when she had so much preying on her mind these days? But Sugna was always there to take good care of her. She was her favourite companion, her soulmate. Perhaps Sugna was her most intimate companion in other lifetimes. Padmini was touched by Sugna's solicitude for her. She would understand all her needs without being told. There always was a glint of concern in her eyes for Padmini. But what she loved best in Sugna was her honeyed voice.

To keep her Ranisa happy and comfortable seemed to be the sole purpose of Sugna's life. Padmini seemed to be the centre of her consciousness. Padmini's mother valued

Sugna's qualities and justifiably gave her the position of being her principal companion.

Sugna walked to the window. She looked out and said, 'Ranisa, did you see something?'

'What, Sugna?'

'Please come here and see for yourself. A long row of palanquins is moving towards the city gates.'

Padmini got up. She saw a large number of palanquins heading towards the gate, where a detachment of the royal army was stationed. Strange sounds came from the movement of the palanquins. The attendants bearing the palanquins seemed to be in a pleasant mood, as if going on a pilgrimage.

Suddenly, there was silence. It looked as though some very distinguished person was about to visit the women's apartment.

Just then Magan walked in and informed, 'Patali Kunwar Yuvraj, the prince has arrived.'

'Patali Kunwar Veerbhan?' She was a little astonished. After seeing his response in the meeting a day before, she feared him no more. But what could have brought him here? She tidied her dress and gently pushed back a lock of hair that had strayed on to her forehead. Then she went back to her armchair.

Prince Veerbhan entered the room. Padmini was relieved when she looked into his eyes. There was no trace of the void she had encountered three days back. The tense expression on his face had relaxed, and he seemed to have overcome his defeatist attitude. It looked as though he had found the right solution to the crisis, as though his despondency had been washed away. A soft exterior with an air of quiet authority—that was his personality. He was simple, yet impatient, and these attributes would not allow any bitterness to stay for long.

Veerbhan was transparent like his father. Even the minutest wave rising in his heart was visible on his face like the reflection of clouds over a lake.

The prince bowed to Padmini respectfully. 'Ranisa, the campaign led by Gora has set off. If everything turns out the way it has been planned, the king will be freed by the evening.'

It felt as if a light finger had swept over a thousand strings, unfurling sweet music around her. *Is it true? Will the Rajan be freed from the sultan's prison?* She looked into Veerbhan's eyes to reassure herself. He appeared to be confident.

Their eyes met, and suddenly, the enthusiasm with which he had met her flickered out. It seemed as if the memory of his last visit had come back to him. Remembering the alacrity with which he had attempted to cut her to the bone the other day made his eyes shine with unshed tears. He silently admitted his mistake and she wordlessly acknowledged it.

When he spoke again, he recounted the developments of the past few days briefly. After she had left, Gora and Badal had discussed the issue and arrived at a conclusion.

After this, they had immediately sought permission to meet the prince.

They conveyed their discussion to the prince and conferred with him in depth on all aspects of the impending crisis. Mahamantri Mahan Singh and Ajay Singh had also been called to the meeting.

'When the mahamantri saw Gora in the prince's chamber, his initial reaction was that of cautiousness. But when he came to know that Rani Padmini herself had visited him at his residence, he felt reassured. Not just the mahamantri, but the entire state knows that Rani Padmini is Maharawal Ratan Singh's favourite queen,' he said. Padmini felt her face flush.

'Gora wanted me to address the assembly,' he continued. 'But I insisted that he was the most suitable person to speak to our leaders. I knew that he had the knack of a certain fervid eloquence in his way of communicating with a cross section of people.'

Padmini listened without offering any comment. After she had met Gora and Badal, she had known that things were stirring. Yet to know the actual sequence of events was riveting. With every detail, she alternated between surprise and delight. She wanted to probe more, know all the details, seek every nuance of the events that had been set into motion. But she restrained herself. She watched the young man before her, the future king. She felt that deep down he was a kind and caring person. How calmly and dispassionately he was relating the whole sequence of events!

Veerbhan paused for a minute. Once again, his eyes were locked on the queen. Her eyes always seemed to stir something in him. He realized that in terms of vivacity, Rani Padmini was no less than his mother, Prabhavati. But as far as equanimity, intellectual prowess and wisdom were concerned, she was way beyond his mother.

He said, 'The first phase of the victory march is complete and now . . .'

'But I didn't hear the war bugle or the war cry.'

'You must have seen rows and rows of palanquins. Didn't you?'

'Yes, I have been noticing that since morning. Where are all these palanquins heading?'

'They are headed to Ala-ud-Din's royal camp.'

'Why?'

'This time, a trap has been laid to beat the sultan at his own foul game.' He lowered his voice and continued in a hushed tone, 'Today, at the crack of dawn, Badal went to meet the sultan as an emissary of Mewar. On reaching his encampment, he sent word that he was being followed by Queen Padmini, who would be given to the sultan as a gift, and that she was being accompanied by hundreds of beautiful women for the emperor's officers and soldiers. Badal told me that when the sultan heard it, he was so happy that he immediately drew a thousand gold coins from the royal treasury and rewarded Badal. Accepting the money, Badal told him that Queen Padmini had a request to make of the Badshah, the emperor. So overjoyed was the lustful sultan that he readily agreed, saying, "Yes, yes. Tell me what that request is. Even if she makes a thousand requests, I'll grant all of them." Then Badal told him that before she became the sultan's consort, she wanted to meet Maharawal Ratan Singh for the last time. The sultan responded laughingly: "The queen has requested for such a small thing? Tell her that she need not worry. She will be given an opportunity to meet her husband."'

Padmini's face showed that she was trying to grasp what he was telling her but was unable to understand. She said in a simple, affectionate way, 'Prince! I find myself unable to follow you clearly.'

The young prince nodded. Leaning forward and looking at her intently, he said in a hushed tone, 'This information is confidential. The less people know of the strategy, the better.'

Rani Padmini looked more bewildered and anxious. Veerbhan made a quick decision. Unless the cover of mystery was removed, Rani Padmini would not be able to understand anything.

Looking around cautiously, Veerbhan said, 'Seven hundred of our best soldiers, fully armed and dressed in women's clothes were seated in the palanquins and dispatched to the sultan's camp. Even those bearing the palanquins are warriors. They have weapons hidden under their dresses. Gora is in the first palanquin. He is dressed as you, Rani Padmini. He has been covered with clothes and ornaments in such a way that nobody can detect it to be a man with a strong muscular body. Surrounded by armed soldiers, his palanquin has been kept under the most watchful eye. The security provided to him is extremely tight.'

Padmini's eyes widened.

Veerbhan paused in his detailed and cheerful description.

Padmini's mind roared with questions, and yet she had a premonition that some miracle was going to happen. 'O Lord Eklingji! Help us,' she whispered to herself under her breath.

The prayer brought tears to Veerbhan's eyes.

'Who chalked out this plan, Prince?'

'This covert operation is the product of Badal's imagination and intelligence. At first, a couple of members were sceptical of the success of this plan. They found it impractical. But Gora, Mahan Singh, Ajay Singh and I did not agree with their assessment. We felt that it could be acted upon. The most important factor was that, at this stage, we were not in a position to launch a direct confrontation. Therefore, we had to find a way out. War is not won by muscle power alone. The power of intellect is an essential element. Lord Krishna had also applied tact and diplomacy. He finally managed to persuade a scrupulously truthful Yudhishthir to speak the untruth because that was the only way to save his army in the battle of Mahabharata. For us, too, that was the only way out. After some time it dawned on them that they were left with no option. Finally, they fell in with the plan and gave their consent.'

He added, 'Though this plan was Badal's brainchild, it was Gora who took the responsibility of carrying it out flawlessly. After the war council meeting, they did not waste any time and set out to complete their mission with a sense of urgency. There was no stopping them.'

'Gora issued detailed instructions with regard to the deployment of commanders on key positions; the level and scale of combat; and the kind of tactical formation of the troops. Each front has been manned by soldiers of proven abilities. Both Gora and Badal are well-acquainted with the fighting skill of the soldiers. They know how each of them will react to a particular situation. There is one commander to lead every twenty palanquins. Mounted cavalrymen moving back and forth are apparently there to protect them, but their real duty is to collect and deliver messages.'

Padmini listened with utmost concentration. Enjoying her undivided attention, Veerbhan waxed eloquent, barely pausing for breath. 'The mission of this entire plan, its preparation and its operational strategy is to free the maharawal from the sultan's prison. Our aim is to attack the enemy with full force and emerge victorious.'

Having said all that he had to say, Veerbhan went silent. The sky had changed colour, from red to yellow, while he was speaking. The sun had cast its dying golden rays over the treetops.

Padmini looked at Veerbhan.

How morose and gloomy he looked that day, and how cheerful and enthusiastic his tone was now. The sweetness in his behaviour had added to the charm of his personality. What a transformation!

'May I take your leave, Ranisa? I came here to keep you informed. I'll go and wait for the latest message now.'

His soft smile, exposing his sparkling teeth, spread to his eyes and overwhelmed her.

'Why do you call me Ranisa? I am your mother. I'll be happy if you call me Ma . . .'

He was touched by her voice drenched in motherly love. He never imagined that such a graceful, magnanimous, kind and affectionate person could be hidden underneath the strong and determined persona of a woman. He didn't say anything, but his expression clearly indicated that he was delighted to hear that.

He smiled softly like an innocent child.

He remained there for a minute, then bowed to Padmini and strode out.

Inside her, the flame of hope and faith began to glow. The mist of dismay and despair gave way to self-assurance. It was as if she could see the bright light at the far end of the tunnel. She felt as though in that light somebody was scripting a message of hope with golden letters.

Her heart soared. She wanted to laugh out loud. Somehow, they seemed to have made it through the intense distress. Victory! That too over Ala-ud-Din, the emperor of Delhi, whose name struck terror in the hearts of people all over Aryavart. The fact that they had chosen to defend their pride, glory, honour, self-respect would rewrite history.

Her mind was crowded with emotions. Where did all this hope and aspiration suddenly spring from? It was getting more and more agonizing to wait for the moment when she would see the Rajan in front of her; freed from captivity. It was excruciating to have to wait to celebrate.

She was lost in reverie. *How will it feel in that moment? How will I make myself believe that the Rajan is free, completely free?*

What will happen when the sovereign ruler of Mewar appears before me? Will I be carried away by emotions and throw myself into his arms, oblivious to the world? Will he hold me tight the moment he sees me? How will it be in that moment of blessedness?

I will tell the Rajan everything, every small detail of what happened from the beginning to the end. How that night of utter disquiet and unease was and in what mental state I went to meet Gora. How he gave his word of honour to come to our rescue, how he reawakened a sense of pride and self-esteem in one and all, and how I anxiously passed every single moment of this long wait. Every breath, every heartbeat itself will tell him what I had to suffer.

She felt an unusual thrill of joy and excitement. Then suddenly, a depressing thought crossed her mind.

All these things are a figment of my imagination, mere expectations. Everything is uncertain at present. What the future holds, nobody knows. The hope that I am nursing has no solid base. What if things do not turn out the way I expected? Till now, only the first phase of the plan has been completed. There's a lot more to be achieved.

Nervously, she paced up and down her room. Caught in an emotional turmoil, she was unable to calm down.

What could she do?

Yes, there was only one way to come out of this turmoil. It was to remember Lord Eklingji.

She shut her eyes and tried to meditate. The sadness that was flowing into her stopped. She began to feel relaxed.

In spite of maintaining complete secrecy, everybody in the women's apartment seemed to know where the rows of palanquins were going and why. A strange uncertainty, balanced between hope and despair, seemed to hang in the air. It was as though all the perturbed souls around were holding their breath. 'O Lord Eklingji! Be kind to us,' she prayed.

Time seemed to stand still as she counted every moment restlessly.

* * *

All of a sudden, an indistinct din rose all around. Padmini was startled out of her musings. It grew into a deafening roar that was still indistinguishable but sounded like an outburst of elation. She wondered what had happened. The fervid exuberance riding the waves of sounds came closer and closer. Her pulse raced. She could not understand what was happening, but it seemed to augur well for them. Shouts of rapturous acclaim were coming closer.

Cries of *Jai Shri Ekling . . . Har Har Mahadev . . . Bam Bam Mahadev* and sounds of kettledrums, trumpets and conch shells tore through the air. The sound of galloping horses coming closer was becoming louder and louder.

Words of jubilation began to resonate in the women's apartment: 'The maharawal has been freed from the enemy's prison . . .'

'The maharawal has started from there . . .'

'The sultan has dismantled his tent and fled . . .'

'Gora's leadership achieved this success . . .'

The citizens were astonished. They were overwhelmed with joy and amazement. History had taken a new turn in a matter of hours. With that, the fate and future of the state had changed.

All this happened so suddenly that nobody was prepared to believe it. Reality dawned on the people slowly, filling them with joy and happiness, and at the same time leaving them wondering.

Padmini felt waves of reviving music race through her veins, through every fibre of her being. She felt as though she housed an unfathomable ocean. Waves overlapping waves, countless waves . . . breaking on the shore of the sky . . . inundating the horizon . . . beyond the vast expanse . . .

It looked as though Lord Rama was returning to Ayodhya after conquering Lanka. The people were overjoyed. A breeze dipped in sweet fragrance was blowing. Their eyes were gleaming with tears of joy. Streams of delight and despair merged and began to flow together.

There was a nameless tremor in the air. The reddish glow of the setting sun stopped short in the sky. The golden-red rays on the treetops seemed to give off the glint of new life to the leaves. The faces of the people gleamed. Their unblinking eyes looked like doors thrown open expectantly. 'The maharawal is coming.' These were the only words being spoken and heard. It was as if the swaying thickets, the blowing winds, the flowing river were echoing this pronouncement. The water, the sky, the clouds were rotating on the axis of a single point—everything appeared to be moving.

All around, people were waiting for their king. The sense of desperate eagerness was tangible.

Hundreds of girls holding gold *kalash*s on their heads and aartis in their hands, with lighted lamps, grains of rice and saffron placed on gold dishes, were standing in a row. They were waiting to welcome their master with the ceremonial ritual of adoration. With the snap of a finger, the subjects of the kingdom had moved from cloying despair to regained self-confidence. The husband of Prabhavati and Padmini was returning safe and sound. It had sent their hearts singing songs of exhilaration.

Blissfully happy, Padmini sat motionless, her face beaming with a sense of contentment. Overwhelmed with joy, she closed her eyes. Her internal world was restless and anxious even if her demeanour was calm and composed.

Finally, the good news came.

'The maharawal will first go to the temple of Lord Eklingji to offer his obeisance. Thereafter, he will visit Rani Prabhavati and then Rani Padmini in their respective palaces, Prabha Mahal and Padmini Mahal.'

Padmini's attendants helped her change and dress up in elegance. They did her hair and applied kajal to her beautiful eyes to make them more attractive.

An announcement was made in a booming voice: 'King of the kings, the ruler of the country, Maharawal Ratan Singh is visiting Padmini Mahal.'

The atmosphere of joyous celebration gave way to an air of discipline.

And then, there he was; the Rajan was standing in front of her. Time stood still. It seemed like ages since they had last met.

An enraptured and overwhelmed Padmini stared at Ratan Singh unblinkingly with an unquenched thirst in her eyes. Ratan Singh was drenched in sweat and dirt. His muscular body had thinned. A thin film of dry flakes had settled on his sore lips with a streak of blood glistening in between. He was exhausted but glowing with pride.

The mark of red sandalwood paste, which the raj purohit, the state priest, had put on his forehead, was intact in all its glory. A few grains of rice and some petals were stuck to his hair. It looked as though a halo of light had encircled his visage. It was this manliness she had dreamed of.

A smile hung on his lips like a painting. With that, the distance time had created between them disappeared.

Blissfulness was writ large on her face. The emotional turbulence raging in Ratan Singh's mind came to a halt. Enchanted, they looked at each other for a long time. Finding her imagination turning into vibrant reality, she felt a gush of hope and inspiration flowing within her.

The maharawal said with a triumphant quiver in his voice, 'What should I say? I have no words.' With Gora on his mind, he added, 'I am amazed. An unbelievable act of bravery by an incredible man.' Emotions of joy, pain, disquiet, gratitude took over his face in quick succession. 'This victory is absolutely amazing. The credit goes entirely to Gora and Badal. They turned into reality what was virtually impossible.' His eyes moistened.

Padmini cast her mind to the many twists and turns of fate. It was the same Gora who had once been ostracized, the mention of whose name was banned in the corridors of the palace. And now, the king himself was praising him with a sense of gratitude.

After a little pause, he cleared his throat and said, 'I am extremely sorry for the way I treated him. There's no doubt that Gora was a man of incomparable courage and valour.'

'Was?' Her eyes widened in bewilderment. 'What happened to him?' Her anxiety reached the height of dread.

Choked with emotion, the king said, 'He made the supreme sacrifice to save the honour of Mewar.' His steady gaze became pensive and he was overcome with a deep sense of gratitude.

Tears sprang into Padmini's eyes. Gora's face, glowing with immense courage, flashed across her mind. A wave of pain swam through the overpowering joy.

What a paradoxical situation!

The maharawal stayed for a few minutes and left, but not before telling Padmini that he would spend the night with her.

Such great honour! This sudden elevation to her status! To be in his exclusive company on this night of victory was to heighten the joy of celebration. *Is it so because the Rajan knows that some credit of this victory is due to me as well?*

The city was in a festive mood. She could see the entire scene of celebration from her chamber. It was for the first time in their life that such an unexpected event had taken place.

Welcome arches had been put up for the victorious army at every crossing and intersection. The façade of every building, the entrance of every house was decorated elaborately, festooned with banners and flags. All the workers and employees were engaged in giving the city a facelift.

The sound of temple bells and gongs was ringing in the air. Lamps in and around places of worship had been lighted. The poor were given charity.

The way their ruler, the maharawal, was freed from imprisonment was nothing short of a miracle. It was a historical victory.

No sooner did the victorious army enter the city than the auspicious sound of drums, trumpets and other instruments rang through the air. The bards—Charans and Bhats—started singing in praise of the king, the state and the brave warriors. The citizens, in hundreds, lined up on the streets, and swarmed on to the windows, balconies and housetops to witness the victory march. They showered petals on the warriors. The air was filled with enthusiastic voices and the fragrance of flowers.

The setting sun lent a golden hue to every object in sight.

Preparations to honour the gallant warriors were afoot. The city applauded in appreciation when the maharawal made an announcement about conferring the highest title of the state on Gora and Badal. The story of their valour spread to every locality by word of mouth.

Padmini became sad. Gora's calm and stern-looking face swam across her mind. She would always be indebted to him. He did not flinch from laying down his life in order to keep his word. 'Gora, bless you! I salute your bravery!' she uttered silently.

The castle of every celebration is founded on sorrow. It is the bloodshed that adds colour to the decor. The pennant of victory flutters because many people sacrifice their lives. The sacred lamp burns because many brave souls die for it.

Gora's prestige had reached its apex. The bards were praising him to the skies. It seemed as if every animate and inanimate object was profusely grateful to him and cherished his glorious deeds.

But it was difficult to fathom the pain that the martyr's widow had to bear.

The idol of a god has to bear countless blows from a hammer at the hands of a sculptor, her father had once said, before it is worshipped. In all the joy, she felt the weight of her tears for a man who stood up and changed the course of the tide. For the man who listened to her when nobody else did, who sought to convince a parliament of men who were ready to pay the ransom of their queen to save a king blinded by fear; to save her; but most of all to save everyone's pride.

* * *

'Ranisa! Badal has sought permission to speak to you,' Sugna informed her.

'He may, Sugna! Ask the attendants to make arrangements for a grand welcome.' Her voice was choked with emotion.

The attendants rushed to make preparations for the aarti. As soon as the women heard about Badal's visit, they came running to catch a glimpse of the brave young man. They waited with curiosity.

Badal stepped in with an aura of a victor. He was still wearing his headgear and armour. There were gaping wounds on his body. The blood that had settled on the armour had turned black.

As he stood before the queen, he took off his helmet out of respect and held it in his right hand. From his face, he looked healthy, balanced and composed. An unusual bliss and a smile of deep contentment had come over his countenance. It was as if Hanuman had returned with a sense of accomplishment after reducing Lanka to ashes.

The attendants greeted him with a ceremonial welcome by performing the aarti. Padmini applied tilak on his forehead. It was difficult for her to not get emotional. Taking a minute to regain her composure, she blessed the young warrior, 'May Lord Eklingji bless you with a long life. I salute your talent. It has the power to infuse new life into people, like *mrit sanjivani*, the mythological herb that restores life to the dead. Today, your inspiring leadership has given rise to a new spirit of courage and fortitude. Badal, may you always succeed!'

There was no arrogance or pride in his expression. Instead, his face displayed a sense of responsibility and contentment. With his head bowed, he said, 'It was all because of the blessings of Lord Eklingji and the grace of the maharawal.' He paused for a while and added, 'But it was your initiative that led to this victory. In fact . . .'

'No, no, Badal!' Padmini intervened with seriousness and dignity in her voice. 'The credit goes to the maharawal, his brave soldiers, his subjects and above all, to you and Gora.'

'I came here to give you a message from my uncle, Gora.'

'Gora's message? Were you with him in his last moments?'

'In those moments, he was surrounded by the enemy. There was no opportunity for him to say anything. We met briefly after the maharawal had left on horseback. He told me "Go and tell Ranisa that Gora has kept his word." He made a request too.'

'What is it, Badal?'

'He said that the maharawal was annoyed with him and requested you, Ranisa, to clear that mistrust.' His tone revealed the pain that had plagued Gora's heart.

What could she say? The maharawal was already indebted to him. He was filled with remorse. In his eyes, no one was greater than Gora. Padmini closed her eyes involuntarily. Gora's stern face flashed before her. Beneath the calm, balanced and dispassionate exterior, Gora had been hiding intense pain. He had always exercised extreme self-restraint and not let anybody suspect the hurt he guarded closely.

But even the most hard-hearted have feelings. Gora felt pain even though he may not have let out a sigh. But there comes a day when even the brave cannot help bursting into tears. Even the mighty Himalayas must have felt some unbearable pain that forced it to break into tears, which had come to be known as the Ganga's descent.

Emotions crowded her mind and brought tears to her eyes. She felt as though she had left behind a terribly desolate terrain and reached a new horizon with a new sun piercing through dismal darkness.

'I no longer need to do that, Badal! His brave deeds have won him a place in the heart and mind of not just the maharawal but of each person present today and also the coming generations.' Her throat felt constricted when she added, 'We grieve the loss of a great son of our motherland.'

Badal said, 'There cannot be any greater honour for a soldier than to lay down his life in the service of his motherland.' His face was glowing with a sense of pride. He waited for a while and then added, 'May I take your leave?'

'So soon? I want you to tell me more about your campaign.'

A smile indicating a sense of achievement danced on his lips.

He started calmly, 'The entire plan was spearheaded and conducted with such smooth coordination that the royal army was caught napping. They had no time to counter-attack. Their strategy was in absolute disarray. There was total chaos in the enemy camp, which led to their grip slackening on the situation. They were left with no option but to flee.'

Padmini was very happy to hear this. 'Tell me more,' she cajoled him. 'I want to know about the operation from the beginning to the end.'

A chair was brought in for Badal. He sat down and continued enthusiastically, 'Everything was executed in absolute secrecy and as planned. Nobody suspected our motive. Drunk with arrogance, they were so confident that they had relaxed vigilance. It made our task of gaining entry into the sultan's camp easier. When we were close to the tent, we sent word to him that as decided Rani Padmini would like to see Maharawal Ratan Singh. Blinded by lust, the sultan agreed without a second thought. Once he was inside the camp, Uncle Gora looked around and inspected the enemy positions.' Badal paused for breath.

Padmini asked the attendant standing by her side for water. She returned with a tumbler. Badal drank it and felt refreshed. Relaxed, he picked up the thread of his narrative, 'Just as he approached the maharawal, Uncle Gora uncovered himself and drew his sword. Before the guards could react, he had severed their arms. Before they could understand anything, Sangram had stabbed them to death. Other soldiers too unsheathed their swords. As signalled by Gora, Sangram Singh took over command on the left while Suwarna Singh managed the right. Bhim Singh was assigned the task of breaking through the enemy lines. The enemy forces, meanwhile, were still unaware of our plan of action and the strategic positioning of our soldiers.'

Padmini's heart was filled with pride and affection for Gora.

'The maharawal was momentarily taken aback when he saw Uncle Gora in that form. He stared at him in astonishment. He was either not able to understand what was happening or he didn't believe his eyes. In the little time that was available, Gora explained the plan to the king and said, "Maharawal, leave immediately, please. We have very little time at our disposal."'

Badal's voice did not show any sign of tiredness even though the military operation had left him exhausted.

'The maharawal thought for a moment and then looked at Gora. The next moment, his mind and feet worked at lightning speed. Escorted by two armed guards, he went to the waiting steed. The maharawal took over the reins and spurred the horse into a gallop. He took the safe route that passes through the dense forest. Uncle Gora's eyes brimmed with tears of joy.'

A feeling of high regard for Gora arose in Padmini's heart, which soon merged with the tenderness of her affection for him. The attendants were listening to Badal open-mouthed, their eyes on him, waiting to hear more.

'As soon as the maharawal left, the royal army grew suspicious and began to shout that they had been cheated. Bhim Singh and Sangram Singh kept the advancement of the enemy soldiers in check. Had they failed to do so, the maharawal would have been hemmed in by the enemy soldiers, in which case it would have been impossible to stop them. The two commanders attacked the enemy camp, killing several soldiers. Strengthened by their warriors, they continued to break through the enemy troops who resisted but were fighting defensively. They were stunned by the sudden assault. Further, the killing of six or seven of their skilled fighters demoralized them.'

Padmini was daunted by the details. Her eyes shone as she listened to Badal.

'The battle was heavily tilted against them. They soon came to know that Gora was leading the operation. They surrounded him as though he was their sole enemy. But with his unparalleled fighting skills and extraordinary swordsmanship, he was able to make his position strong. He was fighting as if it was a personal fight, as though he had only that day to prove his loyalty towards the maharawal, to take revenge on Raghav and to prove his reputation as an accomplished man-at-arms. If one could look at him, it seemed as if he was Lord Shiva and this was his dance of annihilation.'

The more the attendants listened to the blow-by-blow account, the more their hearts were filled with wonder. Everyone hung on to each word, impatient to know every nuance of the attack. Badal's words were pregnant with his courage and fortitude.

'Nisurat Khan, the chief of their army, who had let loose a reign of terror on the surrounding villages, confronted Uncle Gora. He attacked Gora, who swirled immediately and escaped unhurt. But then his left arm received a heavy blow. Uncle Gora flew into a rage. In his counter-attack, he beheaded Khan in a swift motion. Screams of terror rang through the air, forcing the sultan to come out of hiding. As soon as Gora's soldiers saw him, they pounced on him. But the sultan's guards rallied around him and took him away to an undisclosed location. This turned the situation to our advantage. Their focus shifted in an effort to protect their Badshah. We seized this opportunity to mount a vigorous attack. Disorganized without a commander, they began to lose ground.'

As Badal kept up the narration, he relived the moments and was overcome with jubilation.

'While this was going on, the enemy soldiers closed in on Gora and found him alone. But he was alert. He swung around and attacked them one after another. The sharp edge of his formidable sword penetrated their armour and killed them, even as his eyes flashed. Unfortunately, he lost contact with us and died a hero's death.'

Silence descended.

How did he die? How did someone who seemed to have a hundred arms and a hundred eyes succumb? Padmini's heart was torn with helplessness that nothing could be done for the mighty warrior.

'But by then, the situation was under our control. We had pulverized their defence. The sultan probably understood that it was difficult for his forces to match us. His encampment had been demolished. He ordered his troops to flee. They ran for their lives, causing a stampede in which some of them were trampled.'

'It doubled our enthusiasm. We pretended to chase them but let them escape,' Badal said with a smile. 'Some of our soldiers stayed back to perform the last rites of those killed in action. They will also bring back the large cache of arms left behind by the enemy.'

He paused and continued, 'But the campaign is still incomplete.'

The attendants, who were listening attentively, exchanged perplexed glances. What more remained to be achieved?

'The sultan will not sit quietly. Shocked by this defeat, he will launch a counter-attack with greater vengeance. Whether this will happen immediately or after a while, no one can say. But he will come.' As he spoke, Badal's face wore a look of determination.

The attendants, cheerful a moment earlier, panicked. A quiver of fear returned to their eyes. They were uncertain if they should feel elated at the victory or be intimidated by the prospect of the counter-attack.

Padmini knew that Badal was conscious of the impending situation. She did not say anything, but her vigilant eyes were looking at something else.

Finally, she asked Badal, 'Where were you in this campaign? I can see that you are badly wounded.'

He replied respectfully, 'I was leading the second line of attack. In fact, I had requested my uncle to take me under his command. But I was an emissary in his mission of rapprochement. Fearing that they might recognize me, I was assigned charge of the second line.'

Padmini smiled and said, 'Modesty forbade you from mentioning your deeds of bravery, but I know for certain that your incomparable valour reached new heights in those moments.'

'It's my privilege, Ranisa! But it was you who aroused this strength and capability in me,' Badal said with a smile of delight.

Padmini went into her bedchamber and returned with a seven-stringed pearl necklace. She placed it on a silver plate and offered it to Badal. 'This is a gift from me for your gallantry. Please accept it.'

Badal received it with great humility. Bowing respectfully, he said, 'I feel honoured by your kindness, Ranisa! May I now take your leave?'

Padmini nodded and said, 'God bless you!'

Badal strode out. Her eyes followed him till he disappeared. She could not help but say, 'A brave warrior who would willingly lay down his life to keep his word. May he live for eternity!' Tears were flowing from her eyes.

She was moved by what she heard of Gora's loyalty, bravery and valour. The honour of Mewar was safe but not without great sacrifice.

She sighed and called Sugna. 'Go and tell the chief badaran to make arrangements for sending silver platters laden with gifts of fine clothes, gold ornaments, jewels and sweets to the widow of Gora and the wife of Badal.'

'Yes, Ranisa!' Sugna bowed and left.

The opalescent glow of the setting sun fell on the floor; the deepening translucence of the evening began to descend.

The sound of celebratory drumbeats continued to rise. At the temple of Lord Eklingji, the maharawal was being weighed in jewels.

It looked as though a new age had dawned. And the man of this new era was Gora, who had sacrificed his all for the sake of his country and his king.

* * *

The evening was progressing. The darkness of the night began to spread. The sky, studded with the moon and stars, looked breathtaking as though it was vying with Padmini's ethereal charm.

The evening was dedicated to the beauty of Padmini, who was getting ready.

Her attendants entered the room with small bowls of white butter, yoghurt, milk with aromatic herbs, scented water and other unguents. While the other attendants were busy doing one thing or the other, Magan, with her sense of fun, ensured the atmosphere was energetic and celebratory.

Padmini wanted the make-up to be simple and modest. But in this hour of celebration, they would not listen to her. Lakshmi, who was an expert beautician, wanted to seize this opportunity to exhibit her art.

She busied herself in getting Padmini ready. Lakshmi had an excellent collection of rare herbs and other natural products for skin treatment. She knew many home remedies that used sandalwood paste, saffron, musk, turmeric and other herbal extracts. But that was not what she was here for. It was an occasion for her to exhibit her extraordinary skill of applying make-up that enhanced appearance.

Chests inlaid with gemstones, full of fine silks, gold ornaments and jewellery were lying open. Intense discussions were held to decide which dress would suit which colour and which set of jewellery would best match the queen's dress and make-up.

Hours later, after she was adorned with the traditional shringar, Padmini looked divinely gorgeous. A crescent-shaped ornament with pearls dangled over her crystal-smooth brow, a chaplet studded with rubies caressed her slender neck, a garland of twenty-one pearl strings embraced her rounded breasts, and armlets set with jewels clasped her arms. She was aglitter in exquisite finery with gleaming bracelets, earrings, rings and a diamond nose stud.

Her golden ghaghra, red blouse, colourful bodice and red odhani were like the gossamer to her beauty. She waited with her luminescent eyes hidden under long lashes, her luscious tresses waving like the pennant of the god of love, fragrant with the smell of flowers and the parting bedecked with pearls.

Her body, slender as the *malati* creeper, was adorned with gems and jewels. But it was her soft effulgence that stood out against the finery. The luminosity of her large dark eyes outshone the beads of her pearl garland. Her body brimmed with voluptuous youth as though it was a life-like statue of a celestial nymph.

She looked at herself in the mirror and felt as if it had been years since she had last seen herself this way. *Tonight, the Rajan will see this beauty.* A pleasant thrill of anticipation ran through her. A sense of blessedness quivered in her eyes.

The moon hid behind a chunk of clouds, but its luminescence continued to transcend the screen.

The decorated bedchamber stood transformed. Chandeliers, with strings of grape-shaped gem-lamps hanging from the high-domed ceiling, lit up the room. The light from them created an illusion of undulating waves. A wisp of smoke from burning incense sticks spiralled upwards, and the air was filled with the pleasant smell of musk and *agaru*. The bed was strewn with flowers from the palace garden. A rose water sprinkler, a vial of scent and *gajra*s of sweet-smelling flowers had been placed close to the bed. The elaborate decoration befitted the breathtaking elegance of its mistress.

The attendants had left. The tinkling sound of their anklets had receded into the distance. The noisy fireworks of their giggles had faded.

Oil lamps placed in the niches were glowing. The night was soft and Padmini was waiting for her soulmate eagerly. Every passing moment seemed like an age. It seemed as though it had been a lifetime since she had seen him.

Shrubs and thickets, flowers and creepers, groves and gardens were drowning in the gathering darkness. Beads of water glistened like pearls on the leaves of the lily blooming in the pond. Cool air wafted in through the intricately-designed lattice screen of the balcony.

Once, overcome with emotion, the Rajan had said, 'I wonder when I look at you, Padme! You have come from a place of wilderness. Nothing seems to grow there except the stunted wood apple trees and some cactus-like plants. It is an endless expanse of sand and dunes as far as one can see. Long spells of drought have turned the region into a desolate, parched landscape with acute scarcity of water. How did it happen that an extremely beautiful girl like you was born in that dry barren land?'

She laughed at hearing that. Her beautiful teeth as white as the buds of the kunda *flower sparkled. Her smile spread a gleaming light.*

'Our land was not always like that. There was a time when the Saraswati used to flow there. And long ago, a roaring sea did exist there.'

'I don't know what distant past you are talking about,' the Rajan said with a teasing smile. 'When I reached there, the blistering midday sun was beating down mercilessly on us. We were running on the burning sand chasing a mirage. We could not find any trees to offer us shade. After wandering a lot, we finally located a shami *tree in whose sparse shade we could relax. Even that isolated tree, thirsty and covered in thick layers of dust, had lost its natural lustre.'*

A smile flashed on Padmini's face. She looked her husband in the eye and said, 'Why did you take so much trouble to go to that land? What for?' Mischief glinted in her eyes.

'You will not understand, my love. The attraction of a beautiful woman like you is irresistible. But you didn't answer my question: how could a celestial damsel like you be born in that arid dustbowl?'

This time her laughter was louder, her blush brighter. Ratan Singh was soaked in that cascading bliss. He gazed longingly at his tantalizingly charming wife.

'The answer to your question lies in the long history of that land. When Lord Krishna left Mathura for Dwaraka, the gopis, *the cowherd girls from Vrindavan who loved him intensely, could not bear the separation. Their yearning and longing increased with every passing moment. In desperation, the lovelorn women set out in the direction Krishna had set out. Krishna, however, had chosen a different route to reach Dwaraka because in those days the Kalayavan forces had laid siege to Mathura's western border, and the Jarasandh forces stood on the eastern border. To avoid the two-pronged conflict, Krishna took a longer route through the rugged and rocky desert. It took him a long time to reach his destination.*

But the poor naïve women from the land of Braj, deeply attached to Krishna, went astray in the desert and could not find him. They were exhausted. Left with no option, they decided to settle down there. We are told that they were our ancestors.'

The Rajan laughed heartily and said, 'Now I understand. So this exquisite beauty is the legacy of the gopis, Krishna's devotees.' His eyes sparkled with exuberance.

Those beautiful moments now seemed like a dream. That period in her life was full of many such pleasant and sensuous experiences. Any attempt to recall them would present before her mind's eye a rainbow of heart-gladdening images.

The image of the Rajan's face with beads of perspiration on his brow was deeply ensconced in her mind. *How handsome he looked, so manly!* She was bubbling with a yearning to be embraced by him. *Today I will bind him with the cords of love and longing and the warmth of the most intimate feelings.*

The Raj Marg, the royal highway, was lined with streetlamps. Dim lamplights were twinkling in the windows of some houses and mansions. Silence had descended. Only the feeble sound of celebration could be heard from afar.

Sometimes destiny makes us wait for such a long time that a moment seems like an age and a day becomes a *kalpa,* an era of millions of years. Restless, Padmini stood close to the oriel window like a statue. In that ominous silence, something stirred within her.

The glamour and glitter of lavish opulence had dimmed. She was becoming impatient to surrender herself to him.

It was past midnight, but Maharawal Ratan Singh was yet to arrive.

Sugna came and raised the wicks of the lamps and poured more incense into the containers. Wisps of fragrant smoke rose in tangles.

Apprehensions began to flutter in her mind. Sugna could sense the tension but chose to keep quiet. She went back without saying a word.

Perhaps he will spend the night in Prabha Mahal with his patrani, Prabhavati. After all, she is his principal queen. She deserves the highest regard. And this night is special.

But the Rajan had clearly said that he would spend the night with Padmini.

What happened to his word?

There had been no intimation, no message and no communication.

What could be the reason?

She was struggling to cope with the tangled emotions troubling her.

Suddenly, a voice within her said, 'When one is overcome with emotions, every word that is uttered is not necessarily a bond. Therefore, the Rajan is neither bound to keep his word, nor does he owe an explanation to anyone.'

Maharani Prabhavati's image of her self-proclaimed superiority crossed her mind. A part of her felt she was entitled to it. *The Rajan has a commitment towards her.*

Then, a question struck her like the twang of a bow string, *'What about me?'*

The long wait had blurred her thoughts and sapped her spirit.

An unfamiliar void pervaded her emotions. She had everything she could aspire for. And yet there was something that was missing.

Will this night that promised to fill her heart with a sense of pride and glory pass this coldly?

Something akin to a stinging pain rose within her. The beaming smile that flashed on her visage a while ago had disappeared. She felt a shiver of apprehension. Hope began to turn into dejection.

She tried to assuage her crushed soul.

What is so strange about it? Rani Prabhavati has the first claim on the Rajan. She is senior to me both in age and place of honour. She is his patrani and . . .

Beyond that, she found her heart unprepared to concede more generous thoughts.

She was not willing to believe that he would not visit her. She did not want to give up hope and confidence in the face of apprehensions.

Padmini is the queen of his heart. He has to come to me. There is no doubt.

A thrill of joy ran through her.

But why does this thrill lack energy and appear so despairingly solicitous?

A sense of something missing was gnawing at her, but what was it?

Her desperate eyes wandered across the mysterious criss-cross of light and shade patterned by the moonlight filtering through the trees. Her sense of unease grew with every passing moment. A solitary bird separated from its mate flew away from the bushes beyond the pond, crying *kreen . . . kreen . . .* all the way. The darkness deepened. The quietude thickened.

Sugna arrived just as Padmini's wish-fulfilling wait reached its apex. With helplessness writ large on her face, she kept her eyes downcast, as if she would rather not meet Padmini's eye. Padmini stood transfixed. Her heart raced but she kept her inner turmoil concealed. She did not let anybody know what was troubling her.

Sugna spoke in a cold impassive voice, 'His Highness has arrived at Prabha Mahal.'

A crumbling wall came crashing down inside Padmini. But she managed to look unperturbed. She kept her deep breathing suppressed. A muted cry resounded in her head: *'He didn't come to me! Didn't come!! Didn't come!!!'*

The rising wave of exhilaration had been slashed abruptly. This disregard of her feelings had slammed the door to her dreamworld in her face. She was numb with shock. An attack and counter-attack of emotions left her nonplussed.

The light from the gem-set lamps began to dim. Her sense of pride began to erode. The cavernous night of separation began to expand. Winds began to swoosh over the hills.

She had no option but to suffer this agony, this slight. She could not help it. It was not for the first time that she had been cold-shouldered. She had already put up with such inattention on several occasions earlier, she thought.

It felt as if somebody had forcibly taken away all her happiness. She stood staring into space. The stars began to lose their glimmer.

A debilitating despondency began to seep within her, twisting and turning all the way. The wait was interminable.

The royal bed was untouched, unruffled. The flowers that had been scattered began to shed their petals one after the other, the spiralling wisps of smoke blurred, and a fathomless agony began to torment her. The intense pain brought tears to her eyes.

Everything around her was eerily quiet. Thoughts that crossed her mind a while ago evaporated and she was overcome with feelings of inadequacy and low self-esteem. Suddenly, she felt as if she was all alone without anybody to stand by her.

She could hear some woodsmen talking in the distance.

The wheel of time was moving unobstructed. The first phase of the night had passed. It was past midnight.

With that, her longing too had passed.

I am not the only queen with a claim on the maharawal. He must have been faced with the problem of choice. If he had preferred to visit me, it would undoubtedly annoy the maharani. It would be unbearable for her. And he would be extremely perturbed to find the maharani sulking. He would lose his peace of mind. What the maharani wants is important for the Rajan.

The Rajan knows that his Padma is generous and kind-hearted and would not mind if he showed some consideration for the senior queen. After all, one can afford to do injustice to those closer to one's heart. There is some kind of pleasure in bearing such injustice. Such injustice, howsoever bitter it might be, holds in its womb an indefinable self-contentment.

She suddenly wondered if her brooding was her agonized mind trying to find a way out of the restlessness.

The sense of defeat grew deeper. At that moment, deep in her heart, the gap between the feelings of joy and sorrow shrank so much that she found it difficult to set them apart.

Slowly, the skies began to brighten. The world was bathed in the light of the rising sun. Far in the east, a pipal tree wore the pink glow of dawn. Padmini's tired visage lit up with renewed hope. There was no trace of any emotion on her face. There were no pangs of separation or nonchalance, but there was no affection either.

A soft light glowed in the room. Golden lamps filled with ghee were burning. A soothing calm was in the air.

An announcement was made that the maharawal was visiting Queen Padmini. Her eyes sparkled like glittering jewels. In no time, she forgot everything that had tormented her a while ago. A babbling brook of pure, unadulterated love began to flow within her. She felt something like the storm of exhilaration rise in her heart, but she repressed it.

The Rajan stepped in.

Embellished with the valour of a brave warrior and drenched in royal grace, he let out a smile. It stayed on his lips for a brief moment and then disappeared. Looking at him, she was unable to decide whether he was a king or a lover, a person close to her heart or a complete stranger.

Holding his stole edged with golden lace in one hand, he slowly came towards the bed, taking every step thoughtfully. He seemed unaffected by the opulence of the decor. He calmly reclined on the bed with his head on the bolster placed on the white silk sheet. He kept gazing into space.

Padmini felt that he was lost for words. Yet outwardly he was not looking restless or disturbed like before. He looked calm and composed.

After a few moments, he muttered, 'After undergoing the trauma of being confined to a dark dungeon in the painful presence of guards, one truly realizes what freedom is all about. What an irony it is that we are unmindful of this great gift of God.'

He still seemed to be struggling to express himself. 'The darkness and isolation forced me to think a lot. It's true that a person who has never suffered pain cannot understand what others feel. Staying in a magnificent palace, I probably would not have any idea of what atrocity is.'

'It is in isolation that one can discriminate between truth and untruth. All great experiences of life happen in isolation, when one is all by oneself, Rajan!' Padmini wanted to divert from the topic. She knew that the king was an emotional person. He was temperamental and would easily get frustrated.

He took a deep breath and said, 'It was not like this, Padme! In fact, I had lost my self-esteem. Their unjust and inhuman treatment revived it.'

'They didn't treat you as a king?'

'As a king? Huh?' He laughed ironically. 'I was kept hungry and thirsty. They made fun of me. That heartless fiend would order his soldiers to whip me and watch my ignominy with glee. And that evil-minded Raghav . . . he too was there watching with a devilish grin.'

A deeply felt pain shadowed Padmini's eyes.

'It was Raghav who conspired against us by luring the sultan into catching a glimpse of you. He then laid a trap for me. He knew that once Ala-ud-Din cast his lustful eyes on you, he would not stop until he captured you.'

Padmini was thinking that though the king was unable to hide his pain, there was no trace of the usual excitement or tension in his voice. After he had escaped from the sultan's captivity, the king was no more his usual self. A dignified, quiet, mature demeanour had been added to his personality. He seemed to have regained his self-confidence.

The brutalities he was subjected to in captivity came back to haunt him.

'He seems to believe that might is right. He doesn't know that magnanimity, morality and justice are the attributes of a ruler.'

'It is futile to expect such values from him. It is good in a way. The mercy shown by an enemy is more agonizing than humiliation. To tell you the truth, Padme, if he had succeeded in his lustful designs, I would have killed myself. That he would enjoy your beautiful and chaste body is worse than death to me.'

The pain in his words tore a rent in Padmini's heart.

'I am the cause of all that you had to suffer,' she said contritely.

He softened his voice and said, 'No, you are in no way to blame for this. It is but natural that a man cannot resist the charm of a beautiful woman. But . . .'

'It means that beauty is, in fact, a curse.'

'It is not so, Padme! Beauty is the greatest gift from God, it cannot be a curse. Beauty and aesthetic sense have always found a place of pride in our culture and ethos. In our ancient works of art and literature, and also in our philosophy, the central thought is envisaged as *satyam, shivam, sundaram*—the truth, the good and the beautiful. Our great works of poetry have sung paeans of beauty and grace. In our concept of the goddesses, the apotheosis of the aesthetic associated with them evokes a sense of piousness and awakens in our souls the element of oneness with God. The very thought of beauty opens our mental blocks and elevates us to a sense of all-encompassing blissfulness. But minds filled with carnal desires cannot appreciate such spiritual nuances of beauty. For them, a beautiful woman is just an object to satisfy their lust.'

She wanted to take her beloved husband far away from this world of torment, to a place where there was nothing and nobody between them. She abruptly changed the topic.

Padmini felt a new sense of love and a renewed yearning to melt in his arms. Ratan Singh felt her fingers on his feet. He smiled slowly. Padmini could not make out whether his smile was genuine or not.

Ratan Singh was inclined to enjoy this pleasure. However, somewhere within, he was also trying to withdraw from that idyll. In between moments of seriousness and fun, he was lost to the world and wasn't conscious of his surroundings.

Padmini's hands continued to caress his feet. The stiffness in his body began to unwind... the stifling sadness crowding his mind began to disperse... the pleasure of her gentle touch began to soothe his nerves. His eyes riveted to Padmini's face. An inarticulate expression on his face seemed to convey that her face was ever so beautiful; even her growing years had left no mark on her face.

As they say, even an extremely beautiful face begins to look ordinary if you happen to look at it often. But this face is exceptionally awash with a perennial stream of beauty and grace. It appears that the clear sky has bequeathed its blueness to her eyes. A tantalizing streak of love and desire was lurking between her lips.

The conflict in his mind began to dissipate. The deep lines between his brows dissolved. All the tangles in his body and mind began to loosen. The blood in his veins flowed with warmth.

He basked in the warmth of her exquisite beauty.

Padmini had helplessly watched the worried, restless and distracted king for the past few days. *Today, after so long, he's looking composed. His silence looks eloquent.* She sat so close to him that it looked as though a tremulous vernal creeper had found the delightful support of a tree.

Ratan Singh reached out and lowered the wick of the oil lamp to dim the light. This brought them closer. An intimate fragrance caressed their souls. Like a flower-laden vine, her body trembled.

The soft unlit warmth, the rising smoke from the incense sticks, the sweet smell from their lighted tops and a mellow silence pervaded the room.

Lost in thought, Padmini didn't notice when her odhani slipped off. Ratan Singh gazed at her longingly, at her voluptuous body elegantly dressed in diaphanous silks, her delicately sculpted midriff, her lips retaining the innate proud, winsome smile with no trace of trauma, the same liquid eyes of a doe, and her voice as sweet as the mellifluous notes emanating from the strings of a veena. The glow of her face, as bright as ever, radiated only love and yearning, even as irresistible charm dripped from her eyes.

Outside, a thousand moons showered their coolness as though attempting to quench the fire of passion. From far-off woods, beyond the royal garden, came the sound of the joyous peacocks.

An irrepressible invitation in her eyes and in the air kindled a strong yearning in the king. Driven by intense emotion, he drew Padmini into a tight embrace. An ecstatic sense of fulfilment pervaded their existence.

Ratan Singh's weary mind was now relaxed. Hurt both physically and mentally in the past few days, he now found himself in his beloved wife's loving arms. Almost instantly, he fell into a deep sleep. A sense of bliss and sensual satisfaction swept over Padmini's face.

The sweet sound of birds woke her up. She opened her eyes and saw that the night had passed. The king was preparing to leave. He rearranged his stole and cummerbund and walked to the window. Outside, the sun was rising over the distant hilltops. He continued to look in that direction. The king looked calm and composed, perhaps a little pensive. It looked as though he was ready to take on a new resolve with the rising of the sun. As the golden orb rose from the horizon, he bowed deeply, muttering words of prayer. She did not disturb him. There was something changed in the man who stood by the window.

He stood there for a while, and then walked out of the room.

The king had disappeared from sight, but she kept looking in that direction.

She went back to her thoughts. *There's so much change in him. The hard time he faced in captivity shook his self-esteem. But now, he has overcome that sense of inadequacy. The thinker in him is awake. His thinking has found a new direction. Aglow with a sense of real pride, he looks determined and yet is so simple. It looks like some kind of sanjivani, a mythical life-giving herb, has infused a new life-force into him.*

It is so ironic that man does not learn as much from his successes as he does from defeat or downfall. The king's transformation became possible after he went through hell on earth. It was as if that terrifying ordeal was an essential driving force to spur him into action. Mewar, at present, had somehow been saved, but its future was fraught with frightening premonition. Inauspicious stars presaged the state of Mewar. Ala-ud-Din, capable of spelling disaster, had cast his evil eye on Mewar. Having returned empty-handed, he must be mortified. He could attack Mewar any time in order to avenge the humiliating defeat.

The reports coming in from Delhi were ominous and alarming.

After fleeing Mewar, the sultan had been entangled in other skirmishes. The Mongols had made one attempt after another to invade his territory, but the sultan had crushed them each time. The victories made him more barbarous.

Mewar's spies had informed the king that the sultan was preparing to mount an attack. This time, the assault was likely to be worse. The entire operation was being planned under the supervision of Khijra Khan, the elder son of Ala-ud-Din. Khijra Khan was said to have inherited his father's cruelty, brutality and arrogance.

The whole of Mewar was suffused with a new life. The maharawal was sweating blood to save the sovereignty of his state. He devoted every waking moment planning military strategies. The inhuman treatment he had received at the hands of Ala-ud-Din was so fresh that it would not let him be at ease.

Preparations were afoot for the impending war. All possible enemy action was being discussed by the war council. Activities of making and developing arms and other war material had picked up pace. Training sessions were being held day and night to equip the warriors with the skills required to wield the entire panoply of the newly developed weapons.

New training centres were set up. Those already in existence were revived. The war council began to meet daily.

Even those who were not Kshatriyas—those hierarchically belonging to the warrior caste—were conscripted into the army. Chieftains of the tribal Bhil community living in the surrounding villages were taken into confidence. They had always assisted the army of their ruler in times of need. The Bhils, as a community, were known to keep their word. They were experts in scaling steep hills and could easily leap over deep pits and thick bushes. Not just this, they could endure harsh conditions. By enlisting the services of the Bhils, the technique of guerilla warfare was being fine-tuned. Training in cavalry charge, speed-riding, tactical positioning of the forces and other strategic formations and operations were being undertaken every day. Outstanding warriors were appointed as garrison commanders.

Supplies and provisions were stored. The availability of water from natural sources inside the fort was found to be insufficient. Therefore, new tanks were built.

Tunnels were dug underneath the fort. Structures the enemy could use to its advantage were removed or dismantled. Heavy rocks were being stored inside the fort to be used as missiles to impede the enemy's advance.

The citizens of Mewar were reminded of their cherished ideals and goals in order to motivate them to do-or-die for their country. Bards and war-trumpeters, with the magic of their patriotic songs and music, created a charged atmosphere that motivated the people. They girded their loins and got together, determined to face any eventuality in an attempt to defend their motherland.

Tasks were assigned depending on authority and skill.

The maharawal was actively involved in all plans and programmes. This left him with very little time for himself. Unlike earlier, he no longer had fixed meal times or bedtime. He couldn't afford to sit peacefully even for a minute. Finding their king overflowing with vigour, the soldiers and commanders felt a fresh wave of enthusiasm sweeping over them. To sacrifice their all for the sake of their land and their flag had become the sole purpose of their lives.

With their fingers crossed, they were ready for battle.

Padmini was content to see her husband, a monarch, in this new avatar. No more luxuriating in self-indulgence, he was now driven by the mission of accomplishing the mammoth task of defending the honour of his wife, the queen of Chittor. She did not fail to notice that the heat of some fire constantly tormented him day and night.

If only I could play an active role in this campaign! Padmini felt a distinct urge to put her shoulder to the wheel. The river of her life wanted to flood. She was unable to figure out what to do with it . . . how and where to direct its flow? A wave of discouraging sadness took over her soul. She wished she could discard the shallow life that opulence offered.

Am I worthless? Is a woman merely a showpiece, a commodity, an object for sensual enjoyment, a luxurious accessory, someone's private property? Does the very existence of a woman depend upon her being a man's wife or mistress? Does she have no self-esteem of her own without a man by her side? Does she have no personality of her own? Is she helpless and subordinate to men? Are a woman's thoughts and feelings of no importance? Must she need a man's protection for her safety?

In fact, women have been reduced to an instrument to satisfy a man's lust, a part of his repertoire. This is the reason why so many abductions take place; just to forcibly seize that prized possession. This has caused devastating wars followed by treaties between the warring potentates.

Why is it that the nature and attitude of men decide the destiny of women?

Hamir of Ranthambore was a brave king who laid down his life to defend the honour of his land. He refused to hand over his wife and daughter to the sultan. Instead of succumbing to brute force, he chose to make the supreme sacrifice by offering them to the leaping flames. The bodies of the pious women were reduced to ashes but the honour of their souls was saved.

And look how Karna Deo, the ruler of Patan, behaved. Afraid of the enemy, he turned tail and abandoned his queen and daughter. They were dispatched to the sultan's harem. One can imagine how they must have suffered there. The sultan's order was like a whip on their bare souls. It felt as if they were being pushed and dragged to that hell like lifeless objects.

It is male chauvinism that has dealt a severe blow to the hearts and minds of women.

Then why is a woman idolized as Goddess Gauri or Bhawani? Why is she put on a pedestal by describing her as ādyāshakti, the primeval power or grihalakshami, the prosperity of the household?

Her lacerated questions, having lost their voice, went back to sleep in her heart.

The emancipation of women is reined in by men. Sage Manu had ordained that a woman had to be under a man's control from the time she was born till she breathed her last. Did he never feel the need to understand a woman's mind?

Men perhaps do not know that feelings of love and dedication are not precious merchandise that can be bought or seized. Has any man ever recognized a woman's innermost feelings? Has he ever tried to understand her feelings of dedication? Has he ever respected the freedom of her soul? No, never.

A man is selfish by nature. He evaluates everything from his own point of view. It is his own value system by which he judges others.

Why was this persistent curiosity piercing her heart and soul again and again today? Why were these thoughts springing to her mind now, she wondered?

The authors of religious texts do not treat women with dignity. Why don't they think it necessary to revise their treatises? Why don't they realize that, according to the law of nature, the feelings and desires of a woman are as important as those of a man? She too is a conscious creature, a human being with a soul. Why should she be someone's property? Why should a man take responsibility for her condescendingly?

Women are the fountainhead of purity. They are the bearers of culture. But the ancient philosophers and thinkers seem to have exhausted their intellectual energy in giving vent to the feelings of men alone.

Why then do they claim to be omniscient? She felt like telling the authors of these ancient texts, 'You are not human but statues carved in stone that have no feelings.'

Her mind became numb for a while. All her thoughts and questions related to them stopped.

Realizing her position, she sighed. All her responsibilities had been taken care of. *If this is not slavery in the garb of royal protection and care, then what is? Is my education, knowledge and wisdom worth nothing? How painful it is to remain idle after your ambition has been stubbed out and your intellect neutered.*

Padmini wished she could banish herself to a lonely place, away from these stifling surroundings, be all by herself and wander aimlessly.

Outside, rows of trees stood mute with their heads bowed. Padmini gazed at the sun going down behind the thickets. The day had left a haze behind.

Silence hung in the air. A hush had fallen over the tense memories with no scent of the past. The grandeur, the glory, the opulence, the passion of love—all had stopped short.

Winter had gone by, but there was no sign of spring yet. Though the season had changed, not a single green leaf had made an appearance. Everywhere, trees were shedding dry leaves, which made a strange piteous sound. The sky had turned dusty and gloomy.

Where have the cool moonshine of summer, the saffron sunlight of autumn, the rejuvenating rainfall, and the seven colours of the rainbow gone? Is it that our own feelings and emotions lend a particular colour to life?

The trees with their denuded branches wove different patterns of shadows. A solitary *narkat* tree stood bent with unbearable weight. Every morning was burdensome and every evening leaden on her soul.

Festivals, ceremonies and rituals associated with these seasons had lost their verve. Days had passed but not a single song of celebration had been sung in the Ranivas, the queen's apartment. Dancing girls did not swirl to the rhythm of their ankle bells. Earlier, they used to sing and dance with such passion that one would get the impression that the real pleasure was in performing.

But neither the dancing girls' jingling anklets nor the melodious voices of female singers resonated through the hall any more.

A solitary oil lamp burnt in the room. Sweet-smelling smoke wafted up in the air. Padmini, all alone in the room, sat with her head bowed, lost in thought. She preferred solitude these days.

She had partly covered her delicate face with the *anchal* of her pink apparel. More than half her forehead was visible.

The sky had turned deep blue. Night spread its lustrous tresses smoothly.

But Padmini was not looking out. Immersed in a book by the renowned author, Shubhkirti, she read each line with great interest. 'The way during the time of *Pralaya*, the annihilation of the whole world, the city of Prayag remained intact, the *Kalpavriksha*, the wish-fulfilling tree, was unharmed, the same way if during the *Kalikal*, the age of Kali, Mewar will retain its pristine glory . . .'

Every time I read this book, the clouds in my mind part and a ray of light streams in, she thought to herself.

Outside, there was some commotion. It sounded like the palace guards were scurrying back to their positions. In the background, an announcement was made in a grave tone: 'The crest-jewel of all kings, Maharawal Ratan Singh has arrived.'

Instantly, the atmosphere changed into one of disciplined silence in awe of the king's presence. It was after many months that the Rajan had thought of coming to her chamber. *I wonder what drew him here.*

Crossing the columns and the arches, he entered the room faster than she expected him to.

Padmini got up hurriedly. In the process, she dropped the *tamal* leaves on which the book was written. The detached leaves fluttered around before scattering on the floor. It was not difficult for the Rajan to recognize Shubhkirti's handwriting even from that distance. He came forward to help Padmini pick up the leaves.

Shubhkirti, his former teacher, had taught him literature. He had instilled into the king the *samskara*s, the time-honoured spiritual values as enunciated in the ancient philosophical texts. When he was a child, Shubhkirti would hold his hand and take him around various temples: Kaitama Rupa Mandir, Samidheshwara Mandir, Gautameshwara Mandir, Shrinatha and Charbhuja. Sitting for hours on the banks of the Gambhiri, he would explain to Ratan Singh the deeper aspects of dharma. He would often, in the course of his spiritual discussion, break into a song or chant as if in a trance.

Transported to another world, the king was lost in thought.

Padmini shut the door and sat on the bed, close to the king. She began to stroke his hair. The king kept lying indifferently. It was the same room, the same bed and yet how different the king looked!

'Are you tired?' she asked, the cool of the morning breeze in her voice.

'No, it's not so. Just . . . I managed some free time and thought of seeing you.'

He closed his eyes and returned to his thoughts. It looked as though he was wandering in an unknown valley, going up and down desultorily. She gently nudged him off his somnolence and asked, 'What are you thinking about?'

'Hmm,' he said, slowly opening his eyes, 'I'm thinking if it will ever be possible to strengthen peace, tranquillity and cultural moorings in Mewar.'

A shadow of inner conflict came over his face. He had a sense of foreboding that the state was going to face a serious crisis.

In the softest possible tone, she tried to comfort him saying, 'Why do you worry? The people of this land are hard-working and strong enough to endure all kinds of hardship. They have patience. They know how to wait. Once durable peace is restored . . .'

'In the present circumstances, durable peace is only possible in dreams. We have two options: One, we meekly accept the subjugation of that savage and serve him in his royal court, and the other is to oppose him tooth and nail and continue to face untold misery.'

He paused for a moment, pulled himself together, and said in a decisive tone, 'The stage of choosing is past. Now our path is clear.'

Once again, the odious image of Ala-ud-Din's savagery, immorality and treachery seemed to flash before his eyes. He grimaced.

'There is no rule of dharma in his unjust dispensation. What prevails is his fanatic arrogance and his belief in crushing the opponent by hook or by crook. In his military campaign, he would not bother to see if what he was doing was just or not. He murdered his own uncle who was his father-in-law too.' Padmini listened, muted.

He went on, 'Even in his administration, he indulges in injustice and discrimination against those who do not subscribe to his faith. In his state, Hindus are not allowed to keep money and assets beyond the bare minimum.'

'Why should he have any problem with legitimate claims on hard-earned money?'

Retaining the gravity in his voice, he said, 'He thinks that money and wealth beyond a limit emboldens the subjects to revolt. It provides the wherewithal to organize a mass uprising. His political aides have advised him that the common citizens of the state should be ruthlessly pushed to the brink of utter poverty and destitution, so that even in their wildest dream they dare not think of raising the banner of revolt.'

'What I hear is that he proselytizes people of other faiths by force. Is that true?'

'Yes.'

'I can't understand how a person forced to convert to another religion will have any faith in and respect for it. In fact, faith in one's own religion gives true bliss to the soul.'

The king took a deep breath and said, 'I can't believe that the pious and divine soul Muhammad could have taught his followers to adopt this path. What I have come to know from reliable sources is that Ala-ud-Din is not a devout Muslim. He doesn't understand the true spirit of Islam and the Quran.'

With an innocent curiosity, Padmini asked, 'He doesn't have the wisdom or the intent to follow the path of righteousness. He has no faith in his own religion or in spiritualism, and yet he goes on winning war after war. How?'

'Hmm,' he explained, 'the bottom line of our cultural tradition is that life as a human is a mahayajna, a big sacrificial rite. It is on the basis of this yajna that the universe rests. The meaning of the yajna is this: we have to offer all our greed, our desires as sacred oblation into the sacrificial fire. In other words, we have to surrender our all and even lay down our life to the cause of upholding and protecting our long-cherished ideals. But this is not the case with him. He brazenly believes in brute force and unethical means. People like him do not rise above worldly pleasures and the spoils of this world. They would not delve into the mysteries of human existence. Questions of "Who am I?", "Why am I?", and "Where have I come from?" do not churn in their minds. At this moment they have power. They have left their homes and come here not for any spiritual quest but to sack Chittor, which is known for its wealth and resources. They are hell-bent on looting this country as long as they can, as much as they can. Using their strength of power and pelf, they recruit starving men in thousands into their armies and use this force to annex one territory after another.'

'This means our religion is so weak . . .'

The king perceived the question troubling his queen and said without changing the tone of his voice, 'It is not that our religion is weak compared to theirs, or that it makes us weak. The differences that we see between religions are superficial. There is nothing like our God is different from theirs. God is one. God cannot be defined intellectually. He can only be realized through the soul.'

'Why then do people fight in the name of religion?'

He paused, thought for a moment, and continued, 'Our fight is not against Islam. Absolutely not. We are fighting against a foreign invader who is indulging in the most vicious and barbaric acts. He is bent upon destroying faiths and beliefs of those who do not kowtow to him.' His tone remained serious, but there was no tension visible on his face.

He continued after another pause, 'He doesn't believe in respecting the faiths and customs of others. Our sages,

Manu and Yagyavalkya, taught us to give due recognition to diverse faiths and respect the religious sentiments of their followers.'

Padmini listened to him intently. A well-read woman herself, she tried her best to come to terms with what she had heard. However, she could not convince herself how such an evil-minded invader could not be defeated by those who had always followed the tenets of their faith so religiously. Unable to come to a conclusion, she put it before the king.

He responded, 'We have to go a little deeper to settle such doubts. Our way of life is based on certain values, ideals and a code of conduct. The philosophy of karma, as enshrined in our scriptures is so deep-rooted in us that our behaviour is dictated by it. All our actions, both physical and mental, have consequences, which we have to face in our next lives. Similarly, during our present life, we face the consequences of our actions, good or bad, in our past lifetimes. Accordingly, the ultimate aim of an individual is to attain liberation from this cycle of births. Since Khilji doesn't seem to believe in this philosophy, his conscience does not prick him. He thinks he can commit the most heinous crimes with impunity.'

Padmini knew the king was right. She looked thoughtful. The king continued, 'Unfortunately, the wicked Ala-ud-Din is not guided by the true spirit of Islam, which teaches the virtues of love and peace. The meaning of the word "Islam" is peace. Khwaja Nizamuddin Auliya, a Sufi saint of the Chishti dynasty, worked to create an atmosphere of religious tolerance. He explained to the people the real form of Islam. According to him, everybody should try to realize God by following the devotional practices of their own faith,' he added.

'These are matters of religion and faith,' said Padmini. 'But the fact remains that we are a deeply divided nation. In the face of this serious crisis, all the states of Aryavart, big or small, should have joined hands and put up a formidable front. But they haven't. Why don't they realize, or rather why are they not made to realize, that united they will be able to stand up to the invaders and divided they will fall? Nobody will survive. Our great culture, our glorious tradition, our Vedas, our scriptures, all will disappear from the face of the earth.' Padmini's innocent face seemed to have acquired a reddish glow.

Maharawal Ratan Singh smiled softly, as one smiles at the simple curiosity of a small child. 'This is what he is taking advantage of. The internal differences of the Rajput rulers have strengthened the hands of a tyrant, such that his tentacles have spread far and wide. The rulers of this land have never maintained cordial relations. They may pretend to be friendly, but in their hearts they nurse envy and animosity for each other. And since the Turks' occupation of Delhi, all states, big and small, have lost their nerve.'

After a moment's pause, he continued, 'Lakshman Singh, a brave warrior, is trying to get help and support from the neighbouring states. But seeing their present state of mind, he is very disappointed. They are either tactfully skirting the issue of getting involved or trying to dissuade him from taking on the sultan of Delhi. How can they help others when they themselves are in fear and trepidation? All of them have their own axe to grind. They have nothing to offer except dry sympathy.'

Ratan Singh fell silent, but his expressions showed that he had more to say.

'You are saddened by it?'

The sadness on his face was replaced, in an instance, with a neutral expression. He spoke in an enlightened tone, 'No, Padme! I have felt enough sadness. Now it is time I take up my responsibilities as a soldier. I need to be alert and gird myself up to face any eventuality. This fight is not just against a person but against adharma, unrighteousness and injustice as well.'

His face indicated the firmness of his resolve. He regained his composure and said, 'The support of the people of Mewar is my greatest strength. They have become fully aware of the situation and are conscious of their duties in this hour of crisis. Today, in every home there are warriors like Gora and Badal ready to join the force.

She was gazing at the Rajan affectionately. There was no dilemma, no indecisiveness, no dithering. Instead, he was full of unswerving confidence.

'When is he likely to attack?'

'He was forced to retreat last time. He has seen that our soldiers are brave and fearless and our fort is impregnable.

He needs a strong army and sufficient logistics before he can plan an attack, and he needs time for that. This time he will mobilize a large number of soldiers, for whom he has to arrange a huge quantity of arms, horses, food, drinks and other things. And this is a time-consuming exercise.'

He is elaborating the future scenario so calmly. But a flame is flickering in the depths of his eyes. Who knows when this dormant volcano may erupt?

'Let him come with as big an army as he likes. He will have to face strong resistance. Every citizen of this land is ready to sacrifice his life. Moreover, our garrison is naturally fortified from all sides. Since times immemorial, it has been providing extraordinary security to its custodians.'

He was silent for a few moments. But his silence was not static. It was brimming with thoughts. He seemed conscious of the path he had chosen. The path was not easy; it was full of obstacles. 'But the enemy can lay siege to the fort and we can't do anything. It is surrounded by an open field and this garrison on the hilltop is isolated. Although it is difficult for them to get here, they can barricade it to prevent movement of men and supplies. If we are defeated under siege, it will only be because of the blockade,' he said staring into space.

Scared to her wits, Padmini instantly put her hand on the Rajan's mouth, 'Never ever utter such ominous words for Chittor, please!'

This brought a smile to lips. Comforting Padmini, he said, 'Fine! If we win the battle, I will think of shifting the capital to some other place.'

He closed his eyes, took a deep breath and immersed himself in thoughts. With an intense feeling of closeness rising in her heart for him, she said softly, 'Rajan!'

His eyes were closed. With closed lips, he murmured, 'Hmm?'

'When a man finds himself in the throes of insurmountable difficulties, he should, for a while, leave himself in the hands of a loving woman. There have been many instances in the annals of history when people have achieved the greatest successes after they were inspired by a woman's love.' Her voice had the softness of a bird's love for its little ones.

A curve of a smile flashed at the corners of his eyes.

'You are a woman, after all! You know the language of love best.'

She felt as though she had met her loving husband after ages.

He rose to leave.

She watched him go. Every step he took seemed to indicate his firmness in heading towards his goal.

The Rajan has completely transformed. He is an accomplished statesman, politician, leader of the masses, and a dauntless warrior. His voice has the firmness of the Aravali hills. He is not going to leave himself at the mercy of destiny. He has not allowed himself to forget that he was tortured and humiliated by Ala-ud-Din. It seems like the only mission in his life is to take revenge. That unfortunate incident has made him introspective. He has been thoroughly chiselled. All those parts of his personality and character, which were undesirable, stand pared down. What is left is a sense of responsibility, rekindled wisdom and a strong will to wash off the stigma on his forehead.

Having escaped the jaws of death, he felt intensely vengeful. The sacrifice of Gora and other soldiers . . . the pride and glory of Mewar . . . the honour of the flag . . . all this and other thoughts jammed his mind. Never before had he felt such a fire in his belly. Never before had he felt such a strong urge to do or die.

People normally believe that there is an unbroken chain of life from birth to death. But a man is never the same in different stages of life. He changes every moment. With the passage of time, neither the mind nor the body remains the same.

* * *

Samvat 1360 (1303 CE). A midnight in the month of Bhadrapada. It was pitch-black outside. There was no sleep in Padmini's eyes. Her heart beat fast. She tossed and turned in bed with a grim sense of foreboding.

Rumblings of deep, frightening sounds were coming from afar. It felt as if heavy boulders were falling from the sky. Suddenly, huge dark clouds gathered in the sky and thundered. Lightning flashed and struck the surrounding valleys. A fierce storm followed with strong winds and heavy rain. The night was ominously dark. She was scared.

All of a sudden, a tumultuous noise rose from the direction of the Surya Dwar, the eastern gate. It sounded like an earthquake. The next moment, gale-force winds began to whizz past, making the flames in the lamps flicker. The ramparts of the fort shook. It looked as though the universe would tremble.

The entire women's apartment had assembled. Everybody was panicking. With fear in their eyes, they looked like scared fawns being chased by a hunter. They were unable to think clearly. Their hearts were pounding.

The noise became louder.

Ala-ud-Din had attacked.

There was stunned silence inside the fort for a few moments. Everybody was tense.

Soon, the castle reverberated with the sound of soldiers scurrying into one direction. The stamping stopped after the soldiers took positions. The commanders took charge of their formations. Lightning seemed to flash through their limbs. They felt the blood racing through their veins. The *chaturang sena,* the four-wing army comprising the infantry, cavalry, chariots and elephants, were all poised for a fierce battle.

Trumpets were sounded to announce that the army was marching. The tumultuous sound of clarinets, kettledrums and horns filled the air.

The blowing of trumpets and the war cry created enthusiasm among the soldiers who were ready to challenge the enemy. A thunderous cheer went up from the spirited troops hailing victory to Mewar.

Uneasiness took over Padmini. More than anxiety, it was fear, a nameless fear. She paced the room restlessly with her hands clasped together. In a fury of emotions, she put out the lamp in the room and threw open the window. Outside, the rain came down in torrents. Blinding dark skies devoured everything. The storm was at its fiercest with strong winds, roaring clouds and all lanes and roads deep in water.

She looked around helplessly. The figure in the picture on the wall seemed to have smothered her soul. It looked as though the shadow of death had spread all over.

A crack of thunder and a flash of lightning with furious winds made the dense forests appear all the more frightening.

The might of the sultan's forces had increased many times over, both in number and striking capability, compared to last time. Sultan Ala-ud-Din had returned with the sole aim of a bloodbath. He was determined, it seemed, to leave with Padmini this time. He took upon himself the task of leading his army. Khilji, whose name alone had the power to strike terror in every part of Aryavart, was truly arrogant, lascivious, unjust and atrocious.

The command of the army of Mewar was in the hands of Maharawal Ratan Singh. Like any astute commander, he seemed to know instinctively where he was needed most at a particular point of time, and he made it a point to be there. His very presence filled the soldiers with renewed enthusiasm. A signal from him and they happily sacrificed their lives. The morale of the soldiers continued to fly high.

The enemy troops had spread themselves all around the fort, unleashing destruction, sacking and looting villages, and slaughtering innocent people. However, their attempt at infiltration did not gain much foothold. They faced stiff resistance. Every citizen of Mewar was a participant. Villagers, young and old, male and female, ignored their safety and came out to defend their motherland.

The men hid behind bushes and the women handed them spears. These were thrown to target the advancing enemy soldiers. Everyone did their bit to defend the city. They continued these tactics until they could no more check the enemy's movement. When there was no hope left, they cut off the heads of their women and children to save them from dishonour and pounced on the enemy with all their might. This indomitable courage and perseverance earned them victory in many villages.

The garrison commanders remained alert round-the-clock. They kept a watchful eye on every move of the enemy. The army was like an impregnable rock.

The warriors of Mewar were closely observing the strategy of the enemy and had divined that they were incapable of fighting in hilly terrain. Their skill and training in such encounters enabled them to dismantle the formation of the first line of attack. The first-hand knowledge of the Aravali range proved to be an advantage for the warriors of Mewar. A handful of soldiers were able to crush the much bigger army of the enemy.

In the first round, the Mewar soldiers gained commendable success. But the tempo could not be maintained. Gradually, the situation changed. Eventually, it began to reverse.

The enemy troops were so many that they could surround the fort four times over. The long-drawn siege was getting tighter and stronger each day. The rear guard, with their formidable strength, was providing them with support. A fierce battle was being fought around the fort.

A deafening blast rent the air. The upper crust of rocks developed gashing cracks. The entire town was overtaken by mounting calamity.

Action near two gates—Lakhota Dwar and Surya Dwar—and the Chittavari tower intensified. Damages to the fort were repaired overnight.

The attack intensified, making every retaliation devastating. A disastrous chaos with dark clouds of smoke, dust and toxic fumes spread all over as though a volcano had erupted. Men, women and children were buried alive under stone walls and other structures. Cries of despair pierced the air. The spell of death and destruction continued unabated. There seemed to be no end to the bloody battle. The sky appeared to be trembling as it watched the sinister game being played out.

In this reign of terror and treachery, the dividing line between day and night disappeared. Flocks of vultures and kites begin to circle the sky.

The brave soldiers of Mewar had not lost heart in the face of the adverse conditions and lack of men and equipment. They were always aware that the enemy was far more powerful in terms of men and resources. Yet there was no trace of fear, indecisiveness or lack of purpose. As the fight progressed, the sense of patriotism grew.

The soil turned red with blood flowing like water. Everything around, the rocks, the stunted trees were bathed in blood.

The crisis deepened. Misery and misfortune tightened their grip. Chittor, the heart of Mewar, pride and honour of the Kshatriyas, the pivot of freedom, was on the verge of defeat.

At sundown, the fierce fighting came to a halt. The shadows lengthened. The room was dimly lit. Outside, through a wide-open window, the overcast sky, with dark clouds hovering above the hilltops, was visible. The wind picked up. A sudden gust rattled doors and hinges, leaving the mighty walls stunned, alarmed.

The sound of fast pacing steps signalled that somebody from the military camp was coming with a message.

Padmini stepped out of her room.

She couldn't recognize the messenger with his face covered by a heavy warrior-helmet.

'*Khamaghani*, Ranisa!' the messenger bowed before her.

The voice. She recognized it instantly.

'Ajay Singh!'

There were deep gashes all over his body; he was bleeding heavily; his clothes were badly torn.

He took off his helmet and held it in his hand. She looked into his eyes. There was no dream, no hope in them, but neither was there any gloom. The other hand still held the hilt of his sword firmly.

The sun was about to set behind the hills.

'You are grievously wounded.'

'Wounded I am, but not disheartened. I wanted to come to you to keep you informed, but a series of sudden attacks kept me engaged,' he said firmly.

'What is the latest news?' Though her face revealed no emotion, her voice betrayed anxiety.

Ajay Singh replied mechanically, 'On the north front, near the Lakhota Dwar, we have been defeated completely. In other fortifications too we face imminent defeat. On the south front, near the Chittavari tower, we gained some success because of the inspiring presence of the maharawal, but later we had to suffer heavy losses there too. Many of our gallant men have been killed. On the east side at the Surya Dwar, Mahan Singh is holding command. He has penetrated deep into the enemy lines and forced them to retreat.'

'Why are we facing reverses in our campaign?'

'There is hardly any time to analyse,' he replied. After a pause, he said, 'Their superior military strength has given them a huge advantage. When their soldiers fighting at the front are exhausted, they are replaced by the rearguard. We have had no relief, therefore, from the continuous onslaught.'

'Everybody in Mewar, irrespective of whether they are Kshatriyas or not, joined the forces. Why then do have we to face this situation?'

It was not her words alone that questioned him; her tone, her look, her gesture were all poised simultaneously with the question.

'What you say is true, Ranisa! But, in the first place, our regular trained soldiers did not accept this deployment wholeheartedly. Second, we focused only on attack and pressed our entire force into it. We did not think of ensuring reserves to reinforce our fighting troops in an emergency.' She looked at him in anguish. He continued with his eyes fixed to the ground, 'Besides, our arms were too old to protect our men from the assault of the enemy's sharp and sturdy weapons. We have adopted a conventional and outdated technique of warfare against their modern methods and arms. Moreover, we are not used to tackling their treacherous and deceitful ways.'

'Where has Badal been deployed to command?'

'It is because of his great leadership that we have gained success at different locations. The enemy soldiers took to their heels the moment they found themselves face-to-face with him. Those who were unable to flee were put to death. Though he is seriously injured, he has not budged an inch in complete disregard of his safety.

Suddenly, Padmini's heart began to beat fast. Much as she wanted to know, she was unable to get herself to ask about the Rajan.

Ajay Singh raised his downcast eyes for a moment. He could sense the question weighing on her mind. Without any preface, he said, 'The maharawal is in good health and commanding his men bravely and skilfully. Yuvraj, the prince, is under his wing and assisting his father competently. Once it so happened that the maharawal was surrounded by the sultan's men and there was no way to escape. No sooner did their commander, riding a horse, come to strike him, than the prince pounced on the commander like a hawk and struck him with a spear that tore through his armour and penetrated his neck. He fell off his horse. But, unfortunately, before he fell, he attacked the prince with his sword. The soldiers surrounding the king rushed to the prince, but by that time the situation had gone out of their hands and they were pushed back.'

'How is the prince? Is he seriously wounded?' The pain in her voice was acute.

'He has injuries all over his body and his armour has been torn asunder. Our rescue team took him to the medical camp immediately, where he is being treated.'

'How is he now?' she asked with fear in her voice.

'Fortunately, the injuries are not deep. The doctor examined him and gave him medicines. Now he is much better. The bleeding has stopped and the pain has subsided to a great extent. I came here after visiting him.'

'May God give him a long life!' she whispered a prayer.

'The maharawal was there some time back. He also saw the other injured soldiers and asked about their health and well-being.'

The prince's face, evoking sentiments of love and affection, flashed before Padmini's eyes. In her mind's eye she visualized the Rajan taking his injured son in his arms; kissing his forehead; holding his tender hands and placing them on his eyes. Veerbhan was the flame of the Rajan's life and an incessant stream of love flowed in his heart for his son, Padmini thought to herself.

Ajay Singh stood in silence while the queen contemplated all this. Shafts of a blurred shadow crossed his eyes.

He bowed and left.

* * *

Thick darkness began to spread. Outside, the woods looked sad, the skies discontent, the hills helpless and the valleys burdened.

Standing in the dark, she gazed at the ruins. The sight was frightening. Bodies were being cremated in hundreds. The stench of half-burnt corpses hung in the air. The ground was strewn with severed hands and legs. Stacked in one corner was a heap of bones and ashes.

She felt as though the unfulfilled aspirations of the dead were floating around her.

Is this the same place where, not long ago, rejoicing pairs of geese and cranes lazed around in the pond; besotted bees sucked nectar from the sweet-smelling cluster of flowers; poets, in the cosy auditorium, regaled the audience with their poems; Prince Veer practised archery; pious Brahmin women strolled?

How dreamlike is this life! It is as if 'yesterday' did not exist, and this day will also not be there tomorrow. How things have changed. Try as you might, you cannot find any relic of that past. Where have those days gone? Now there is nothing left except a tale of sorrow.

Hazy, serpentine streaks of smoke emanating from the funeral pyres rose into the air as though the souls of the bravehearts who laid down their lives were seeking their final destination in the vast expanse of outer space.

Around the burning pyres was a glow of fire, beyond which the darkness was thick, dense and solid. It seemed like the agony of this place had become one with the tormenting darkness.

An impenetrable stillness stretched all over.

Chittorgarh, which till the other day was the pride and glory of the entire Rajputana, which had been the home of peace-loving and religious-minded people since times immemorial, which had the blessings of sages Shilarya and Harit stood severely wounded and humiliated. Its glory and reputation had suffered innumerable lacerations. Now, it stood as a mute testimony to the all-consuming flow of time.

'O creator of this world! You have created this world so beautifully with your own hands. Why is there so much pain and suffering in it?' she uttered indistinctly.

'What has happened to this life, this land, this world?'

There were no answers.

'Once shining crowns now stand tarnished. Once the pennant of glory is now lying uprooted. Once the rulers of the land now stand vanquished. Trumpets once sounding in celebration of victory have fallen silent.'

The ominously dark night became darker.

* * *

The battle turned even more ferocious. The pressure from the enemy continued to mount. Boiling oil, fireballs of burning oil-soaked cloth and stones rained down on them, but the indomitable demonic forces rose like an ocean. Attacks with swords, arrows, spears, clubs and other deadly weapons continued from both sides. Fountains of blood spurted from severed limbs. All over, there was an eerie sight of blood and gore.

There is always a huge gap between what man plans and the destiny he meets.

The situation was turning grimmer. Supplies began to deplete. Water levels in ponds and wells began to dip drastically. Medicines fell short and the arsenal of weapons was fast emptying.

The boundless courage and fortitude of the soldiers and their commanders began to give way. They began to lose their hold on all fronts. Surya Dwar, Hanuman

Dwar, Lakhoti Dwar and Chittavari tower were captured by the enemy.

Women jumped into wells with their children. Detachments of troops were being killed one after the other on the battlefield. The pillars of strength of Mewar began to fall. Mahan Singh, Bhim Singh, Sangram Singh, Bagh Singh, Bhawani Singh, Krishna Das, Bhojraj and many others met their heroic end.

With their fall, the feeling that they were indefatigable was shattered. The magic was gone. The unchallenged dominance of the Guhil dynasty, which had stood since eternity, came to an embarrassing end. The triumphal glory of their kingdom had sunk deeper into the mire.

One-third of their territory had been occupied by the sultan's forces. Resistance was becoming weaker and weaker. Lack of adequate resources and manpower had brought Chittor in the grip of an insurmountable crisis. The task of leading the defence fell on Badal's shoulders as there was no other senior commander left to take up the responsibility.

A terrifying explosion was heard from the south side as though a meteor had fallen from outer space.

The thunderbolt-like sound was followed by a frightening uproar. With the screaming of several people, the sound of several pitchers breaking was heard.

Prince Veerbhan had died a hero's death. The future king of the Guhil dynasty had been killed in action.

Everyone in the *antahpur*, the women's apartment, was weeping bitterly.

Padmini trembled from head to toe in shock. She felt as though a thousand-pronged sharp weapon had pierced her heart.

The prince's angelic smile glowing with pride, his innocent young face, his radiant forehead, his sparkling eyes came before her.

The centre of the maharawal's thoughts, the flame of his hopes and aspirations, a part of his soul, his beloved son was no more.

She thought of Prabha Mahal, the palace of Maharani Prabhavati. She shuddered to imagine how the maharani must have received the news. The apple of her eye, her son, dearer than her own life, was gone. It was hard to believe.

Silent tears streamed down her eyes. Memories hovered in the dark galleries of the mind like birds with clipped wings.

Atop Chittavari hill, the sultan's tattered flag fluttered. Enemy soldiers could be heard cheering in the farthest corner of the fort. The terrifying noise of their laughter was echoing through the corridors of the palace. The deserted streets, lanes and by-lanes were haunted by the fearful and brutal enemy.

The rudders of Mewar had become so fragile that there was no knowing when its boat would sink midstream. All hopes of winning the battle had been dashed. The fall of Chittor was imminent.

All this while, the enemy continued to get reinforcements to launch even more deadly attacks.

Another painful piece of news came in: Badal had been killed. He had fought till the last drop of his blood. Mewar had lost its last most valorous warrior. Everybody in the women's apartment remembered him glowingly; they admired him as an invincible warrior. Sounds of smothered sobs began to rise.

The garrison had lost most of its brave men. It seemed as though it had become lifeless. Just a handful of senior officers were left to face the sea of the sultan's forces.

Defeat after defeat. Setback after setback. Destruction after destruction. However, the maharawal had not lost an iota of his vigour. The life force in him was as dynamic as ever. Also, deep inside somewhere, there was an intense feeling at work: 'One who sacrifices all for the sake of a cause never perishes. He is immortal even after his death. Only such brave souls rule the hearts of people.'

Maharawal Ratan Singh held a meeting with his advisers, including warlord Lakshman Singh, Ajay Singh, Bal Hamir and a few other commanders. Once again, a new plan of action was chalked out and new decisions taken.

They still had a fire burning in their hearts.

* * *

Sugna brought news from a source outside. It was difficult for Padmini to guess anything from her face. So distressed was she that nothing sounded shocking any more. She had lost the curiosity to hear what Sugna had to say.

But she had to listen to her. She had to make an effort to concentrate. She tried to stay expressionless, but failed to do so.

Sugna spoke unemotionally, 'Bal Hamir, the successor of a small branch of the Guhil dynasty endowed with the title of the Rana, has been declared the future ruler of Mewar after Maharawal Ratan Singh.'

A faint image of the boy flashed before her eyes for a moment. She sat silently.

Sugna reported the council's decision verbatim, 'After analysing the circumstances, it was decided that Hamir be anointed as the crown prince and sent to Sisod, the original jagir of the Ranas, along with some warriors under the guardianship of Ajay Singh, so that in the future he can regain Chittor by mobilizing forces and building military power.'

'There's another piece of information.'

'What's that?' asked Padmini incuriously.

'Before leaving for Sisod, Ajay Singh will bring Hamir to you to receive your blessings.'

Something stirred inside her. She was no more impassive. There had been some reaction inside her.

'When will they come?'

'They should be here any moment.'

Sugna began to tidy up the room. The new crown prince of Mewar was about to arrive.

The other day Prince Veerbhan was here. How everything has changed. Today she will see the new yuvraj.

Emotions dashed inside her heart like waves upon the shore, reflecting their hues and then receding into unknown depths of her heart.

She heard footsteps coming closer.

Sugna raised the curtain of the room.

Ajay Singh and Prince Hamir entered. Both of them bowed before the queen.

Hamir was now the anointed prince.

Padmini looked at Ajay Singh. He was fully armoured. A huge shield was tied to his back. Tucked in his cummerbund were two swords, one each on either side of the waist. He was holding an iron helmet in one hand. His eyes were not dreamless like before. A tiny glimmer of hope rested in them. His persona presented him as a brave and fearless protector.

Padmini's gaze moved to Hamir and stayed there. Mustering all her hope and happiness, she said, 'Victory be to the future king of Mewar!'

The young prince was wearing royal headgear with a jewelled crest on it. His forehead was adorned with tilak. A pearl necklace was hanging till his waist. She looked at his face searchingly. He wore the dignified demeanour of the royal lineage, the radiant glow of the rising sun on his face. She looked into his eyes and felt her heart lift in the fearlessness and clarity in them. The soft pink lips were countered by a determined chin. It was after many days that Padmini began to see things clearly. The young prince seemed to be filled with pride and enthusiasm. Charmed by the captivating presence of the young prince, Padmini took pleasure in watching the gestures of his hands, the little movements of his body, and the expressions on his face closely.

Conscious of his official position, he said, 'I have come here to seek your blessings, Rani Ma!'

The word 'Ma' melted her heart. She wished she could run to him and envelope him in an embrace. But she reined in that emotion.

What do I tell him when there is so much to say? She was quiet for some time, searching in her heart for a gift of words. Then she said, 'In the Gita, Lord Krishna addresses the moral dilemma of Arjun who is loath to go to war. He says: *kshudram hridayadaurbalyam tyaktvottishta Parantapa,* which as you know means "rise with a brave heart and destroy the enemy completely". He further says: *swadharmapi chāvekshya na vikampitumarhasi, dharmyādhi yudhāchachhreyoanyatkshatriyasya na vidyate*; you should not vacillate as it is against your dharma, and that for a Kshatriya there is nothing greater than a war against evil. Being a Kshatriya, you are a born warrior and therefore, it is your duty or dharma to fight your enemy who is *adharmi* or unrighteous. *Nāsato vidyate bhāvo nā bhāvo vidyate satoh:* nothing is permanent or imperishable. Childhood, youth, old age, this body with all its wealth, the sea, the river—all are ephemeral. They are not real. What is real is that which is eternal. And what is eternal or everlasting is the fame and glory you earn by your valour. It is your good and evil deeds that live after you.

'In every age, asuras or demons are born. In the Satyuga, it was Hiranyakashipu, in the Treta it was Ravana, and in the Dwapara it was Jarasandha and Kansa who were demons. But in every age, great men have descended to destroy them. For the Kshatriyas, there is no holier yajna or sacrifice than fighting the enemy in war. The bravehearts hold sway over the battlefield. The stream of blood that flows during a war is the wish-fulfilling *purnahuti*, or the final oblation. The battleground is the receptacle of the 'havi' or offerings as oblation for the sacrificial fire. He who shows exemplary gallantry in war is the recipient of the fruit or reward of a sacrificial rite in which *dakshina* of immense value is offered.'

Hamir listened attentively, respectfully. He was conscious of the fact that she was preparing him physically, mentally and spiritually for the challenges that might appear in his life. His face glowed with immense satisfaction.

After a pause she continued, 'The heavy responsibility of preserving and protecting the pride and honour of Mewar rests on your shoulders henceforth. In order to be able to take up this onerous responsibility, you have to sacrifice your selfish needs and shun the life of luxury and ostentation.'

The queen continued to speak with great emotion, 'Even if you have to live the most austere life, surviving on just wild fruits, sleeping on a bed of dried leaves, you will never make any woman a pawn on the chessboard of your political ambitions. Unfortunately, some rulers are so vicious that for fear of facing defeat and losing the life of opulence, they have given away their daughters to the invaders to be thrown into their harems. That too with no qualms. There are others who have shamelessly chosen to lick their boots, bartering their self-esteem with their favours.'

She looked at Hamir and saw that he was hanging on to every word. She sensed that he wanted to say something but felt short of words to articulate it properly.

'I hope you understand what I mean.'

The concern and affection in her voice touched him. His eyes sparkled.

He nodded and moved closer to her, feeling energized in the protective shade of her love.

'I will pray to the Almighty: May my Hamir be so powerful so as to destroy the enemies of the state completely. May he achieve his cherished goals and be the protector of this land and its flag.'

Overwhelmed with emotions, she added, 'May you become the ideal of the patriotic people who love their freedom! May people of the world remember you as long as freedom and struggle is honoured in this world . . .' And then she was done.

Padmini suddenly felt tired, as if she had been emptied of all that was good in her. A flicker of pain showed on her face. Hamir was looking at her with childlike innocence. He had never before experienced such love and trust.

When he spoke, it was with the gravity of a person beyond his age, 'I swear by Ma Padmini that I will not rest until I finish our enemies off the face of the earth.'

Once again, his addressing her as 'Ma' sent a ripple through her being and reverberated inside her for a long time. Ma . . . Ma . . . Ma was the only sound that filled her heart. The small icicle of maternal love grew into a stream that flooded her soul. Unable to control her feelings, she held her arms out and Hamir walked in. Overwhelmed, she felt as though she was floating in the river of eternal love and bliss.

The darkness inside her was dispelled. She was a complete woman now. Her life as a human being had a sense of purpose. She felt as though what she had lost many lifetimes ago had been returned to her.

As soon as she became conscious of Ajay Singh's presence and of her own emotional state, she checked herself. She had to make some effort to change her expression and look normal.

She turned to Ajay Singh and said, 'You are an experienced warrior. You have to teach Hamir the art of warfare just the way Bhishma taught Yudhishthir the techniques of fighting the opponent.'

'I will, Ranisa!' Ajay Singh assured her.

'To protect Hamir's life is also your responsibility. You understand how important his safety and security is given the circumstances.'

'You needn't worry. I will protect him even if I have to risk my own life. It is my sacred duty to protect him.'

He explained to Padmini their strategic advantage: 'The natural conditions of this area are mostly in our favour. There are many ruins and caves in the vast forest of the Aravali hills. These caves are so huge that thousands of people can be accommodated inside. They have small holes as well to facilitate ventilation and sunlight.

'The high altitudes and serpentine tracks can be dangerous for those who are not familiar with the terrain. The enemy troops trying to enter the area will be visible from above and can be killed or repulsed by shooting arrows and rolling boulders down the hills.'

He reassured her, 'Also, there are a large number of fruit trees and plenty of firewood. The area has many ponds and abounds with precious minerals and metals. There is no cause for concern. Besides, the state's treasury has been shifted to undisclosed locations. Essential material, documents and maps are in safe custody.'

Then he fell silent.

An unknown hope set her mind to rest. She gazed at him, but there was no trace of fear on his face. His eyes were shining like that of a lion cub. She could sense that the blood of a braveheart was coursing through his body.

She went up to a table and picked up a gem-studded sword lying on it.

She came back to Hamir and offered it to him. 'Accept this gift from me, Yuvraj! The red gem on it is the symbol of enthusiasm and vigour in your life. Remember, those who take the trouble of crossing deep gorges alone reach the mountain peaks.'

Hamir accepted it with the dignity of a crown prince.

'May you be blessed with power, piety and long life! May Lord Eklingji protect you.' She felt a surge of emotions. She had to swallow hard as she added, 'God comes to the rescue of those who follow their dharma assiduously.'

'Do we have your permission to leave, Ranisa?' asked Ajay Singh.

Padmini raised her hand to bless them. A smile displaying her maternal affection quivered on her face.

'Let's go, Hamir!'

Hamir bowed and left with Ajay Singh. Before he disappeared from view, he turned and threw a childlike glance at her. A reassuring smile danced on the corner of his lips as if to say: 'You don't have to be terrified by the challenges ahead of me'. His stately gait bespoke self-confidence.

Soon they were out of sight. Just like the pink glow remains in the sky after sunset, the sound of their footsteps continued to linger in her ears.

But even after she could no longer hear them, Padmini was flooded with maternal love. She continued to look in the direction they had left in. She recalled the look on his face when she had blessed him and the reassuring smile when he turned to look at her. She closed her eyes and was soon lost in the comfort of his presence when she had embraced him. Unintentionally, she smiled and beads of tears from her eyes dropped to the ground.

The sun disappeared. A pink glow remained.

* * *

Suddenly, heart-rending cries and wailing from the palace tore into the air.

The king had been killed on the battlefield.

Maharawal Ratan Singh, the king of Mewar, the last ruler of the Rawal lineage, was dead.

An era had ended. The sovereign power had been eclipsed. The thick shadow of all-devouring despair and despondency descended all over.

A wave of grief swept over the women's apartment. Everybody was weeping uncontrollably. Grief-stricken Sugna could not raise her head. She had pressed the hem of her dress over her mouth in an unsuccessful effort to check the unceasing flow of tears, but her hiccups were unstoppable.

Who would tell the queen? Who would console her? What could one say to her?

In a state of shock, Padmini was listless. She looked unmoved, unaffected, without emotions or sense of judgement, thoughts or sensation. She was lifeless like a stone, a body without soul.

Suddenly, she felt pain in her lower abdomen. It felt as if her heart was sinking and her ears were buzzing. And then, a shooting pain arose as if a poison-dipped arrow had pierced her heart. The excruciating pain rose up to her larynx. Tears flowed silently from her eyes.

The memories of moments of joy tore through the cloak of gloom and dejection and came alive once again. Those days when her beloved husband was always by her side played out in front of her. Those intoxicating nights they spent in each other's arms, those moments of love, the unforgettable charming smile, each and every incident, and the memories associated with them flashed before her eyes.

It was difficult for her to believe that the Rajan was no more. She had a feeling that he would come to her with some good news any time.

* * *

The wind was drifting in all directions, weighed down by the wailing of a woman separated from her husband.

The army of Sultan Ala-ud-Din was spreading like wildfire, like a flame with a thousand tongues, destroying everything in its way: men, the sturdy walls, the iron gates. The army was at the main gate. Rejoicing wildly, they were shouting. There was fire and smoke everywhere.

The atmosphere was stifling. The splendour of Chittor had been reduced to ruins. The vestigial remains of the stately buildings and the leafless trees stood like mute spectators of the invader's sport of destruction. The landscape was barren and desolate.

In an attempt to boost the morale of the soldiers, the Ranas of Sisod were crowned and anointed one after another. One by one, they appeared on the battlefield and laid down their lives.

Kal, or time, in its most horrendous form was staring them in the face. There were no options left. Preparations for the last sacrifice had begun inside the fort.

All goods and assets were being collected to be offered to the god of fire, so that there was nothing left for the enemy to take. Married women were preparing for jauhar. The surviving warriors dressed themselves in saffron robes and were readying for the last fight. Bracing for the end, they had pain, anguish and agony in their hearts. However, they were driven by a unique sense of self-respect.

Elephants, horses and camels, who were reared with a lot of care and who were as dear to the warriors as their own children, were beheaded. The mute animals submitted themselves at the altar of sacrifice, bowing their heads as though they were conscious of the defeat.

All the gold, silver, diamonds, precious gems and jewels, and all valuables were offered to the fire as the wood crackled and spat. The ear-splitting sound of things falling and breaking was frightening. Solid metal melted and turned into liquid. The flames rose higher.

In no time, everything was reduced to ashes. Only the glow of the burning fire remained.

A large number of pyres with logs of sandalwood were being prepared on an open ground between Samidheshwara and Bhimtal.

The prospect of losing their nearest and dearest had left everybody with a piercing sadness. Who would console whom? Death was staring at all of them. Everything and everyone lay scattered like creepers without support, uprooted and lifeless. They had wept so much that there were no tears left.

They gazed listlessly at their ransacked dwellings. Not long ago, tastefully furnished and decorated, they used to reverberate with sounds of love and affinity. How frighteningly stark they looked now!

The heartland of Mewar had witnessed many ups and down. Innumerable waves of victory and defeat, days and nights of love and longing, and of pangs of separation had swept over it and receded. In a few moments, everything would be finished. There would be nothing left.

Preparations for the jauhar had started.

Articles of worship used in the yajna had been brought to the venue. In a big vessel, the items required: yoghurt, rice grains, ghee, *modak*s, garlands of white flowers, firewood, *dhoop*, *deep* and *naivedya* had been placed. Urns filled with water were placed on small platforms.

Padmini sat impassively, deep in thought, unmoved like the flame of a lamp that has stopped flickering. All agonizing memories had been erased and a peaceful brightness lit up her face.

She had her family deity in mind. The hazy image was becoming clearer.

A huge lotus flower with countless crystal petals is blooming on the highest peak of Mount Kailash. Sitting on it is Lord Shiva with his consort, Uma. Serpents are slithering around his neck. On his head is the moon, and the Ganga is flowing from his matted locks. Wearing tiger skin as a loincloth, he is holding a trident, a damru *and a* kamandal *in his hands. Devotees are offering him leaves of wood apple, petals of flowers, sandalwood paste, fruit and water.*

Padmini felt piety coursing through her, transcending time and space and entering her soul. She felt her soul expanding so much that her consciousness of having a body was lost.

She prayed. 'O Lord Shiva! Sati burnt herself to uphold your honour. Hoisting her burnt body on to your shoulder, you performed the tandava and upheld her honour. Today, your Padma has lost all her power. Only truth is the power of this powerless. If my truth is as true as you are, then protect my truth . . .'

Sugna came and saw Padmini sitting like a lifeless statue. She shook her gently. 'Ranisa!' she said. There was pain and helplessness in her voice.

Padmini opened her eyes slowly. There was a strange emptiness in them. It was difficult for Sugna to penetrate that look. Tears spilled from her eyes.

'Everything is finished,' she said, drawing a shuddery breath.

Padmini raised her eyes. When she spoke, her voice seemed to come from an unfathomable depth, 'After everything is finished, what little remains is the meaning of life.'

Suppressing her pain, Sugna began to unbraid Padmini's tangled hair. As she touched the queen, she felt her hands ache. Her eyes, bereft of sleep and filled with tears, were red and swollen.

Padmini had to make an effort to turn towards Sugna. With affection in her eyes, she asked, 'You are still not free from this attachment?'

'No, what use is this attachment now?' Sugna responded, trying to take charge of her emotions. As she recalled the maharawal's last words: 'Destiny has given us only this much association with you people,' she burst into tears. She covered her face with her hands and wept bitterly.

'Control your feelings, Sugna!' Padmini's voice was softer. Suddenly, she let out a laugh. It was no ordinary laugh. It was a dry sound that seemed to come from the dark recesses of time.

'You know, a pious woman is called sati. It refers to one who sticks to satya or the truth. And in order to adhere to the truth, we have to undergo suffering.'

Sugna looked at her helplessly. Padmini's eyes held a faraway look as she continued, 'There was a time when I believed that the sentiment of love is the only truth because we think it gives us happiness, joy and contentment. But it is not so, Sugna! It is just an attachment; an illusion. It is all a myth.'

Her eyes were fixed on some inaccessible point. Her voice sounded like the echo of a rivulet gurgling through a cavern. 'This body has to give up sooner or later. One who comes has to go. This life is transitory. Whatever you can see in this world has developed from some root. It will go back to the same root. The entire light, the consciousness, the vital force—everything is a gift from God. Death takes away everything and returns them to Him.'

Sugna made an attempt to say something, but broke down instead.

Padmini's face reflected a divine sense of peace and tranquillity. 'Though this life is transitory, the atman or soul is immortal. As the Gita says: *antavanta ime dehanityasyoktāh sharīrinah*. When we realize this truth, we stop grieving. Today is *mukti parva*, the auspicious day of liberation of the atman imprisoned in this body, an hour of absolute bliss.' Her eyes closed as though she could see everything clearly. Her voice was like a gentle breeze.

Sugna seemed to flounder around the abstruse philosophy. But she did feel some awakening within her, which blew away the dark clouds in her mind. Slowly, she came out of the unbearable trauma.

'Human beings are closest to God when suffering is extreme. Now, remember God who is present everywhere; from whom this universe is revealed and in whom it will ultimately dissolve. Remember Him and realize that these worldly miseries are insignificant, that the fear of death is false. Death is not the end, it is final liberation. And liberation is blissful.' Her words resounded through the empty chamber.

There was a blissful smile on her face.

Sugna collected herself. She remembered the purpose of her visit.

'You've to proceed for your last bath, Ranisa! The place is some distance away.'

Padmini remained quiet with all her thoughts and emotions deep within her heart.

* * *

Colourful apparel, glittering ornaments, aromatic unguents, herbs and oils had been neatly arranged in large plates. Like heavy clouds about to rain, the attendants smothered their tears and prepared for the final bath. The sorrow was palpable. Their faces, dull from crying unstoppably, added to the grimness of the atmosphere. In grief, even the verdant beauty of the forests and gardens had lost their lustre. The grieving denizens of the palace felt as if even the lifeless rocks were crying.

The Gomukh Kund had retained its pristine glory. Clean, transparent and cold water cascaded into it. The ripples carried the reflection of the dark clouds. On the banks of the pond were beautiful ghats where people took their holy baths. The branches of the trees around the pond were bent towards the pond. The steps leading to the water were strewn with flowers and pollen.

Chand walked up to Padmini and sobbed, 'Please bathe, Ranisa!'

Once again, all the attendants started crying together. Padmini, who had become weak from leading an austere life, was the only one without any tears.

She walked with her usual slow gait and descended the steps to take a dip. After she had bathed to her heart's content, she came out. Dripping clothes covered her emaciated body, her lustrous hair reached down to her waist. She looked divine. She turned her neck to one side and tossed her hair back. Dark like the clouds, it splashed beads of water around.

After her, all the other women went into the pond.

The cold water dispelled the mist of sadness. Their weariness had eased and their hearts stopped crying. Each one of them experienced an amazing sense of wellness. They felt as though the holy stream had purified them.

Some birds sing a song of death before they die. They seem to receive some mysterious signals from the divine source and, as if on cue, start singing and feel content. Something similar happened to the women attending to Padmini; they felt rejuvenated as if they had transcended the realm of death.

Padmini looked like a celestial maiden who had bathed in the heavenly river and was rambling in the exotic world of stars and planets beyond the limits of time and space.

She was adorned with her last and final shringar. She was dressed in her wedding ensemble: red embroidered ghaghra, *kasumal kanchali* and yellow brocade odhani, a bindi on her forehead, her hands decorated with henna, her feet coloured red with *mahawar*. But today, the aesthetic sense worked into this shringar was different; its sensuous feel was as different as the emotions invested in them.

The pyres had been decked up.

The venue of jauhar had become a place of pilgrimage: a *triveni* of love, separation and sacrifice. A divine charm radiated from the faces of the women as though they had drunk the elixir of immortality. Tearing through the shadow of death, their eyes could see countless lamps with steady flames shining light on the mysterious truth of life.

Seeing the effulgence of colours, it was difficult to decide whether it was the celebration of the end or beginning of life.

Rani Padmini arrived.

Just then, Maharani Prabhavati came.

Padmini's eyes turned towards the maharani and stayed on her for a while. Today there was no arrogance, no malice, no itch to humiliate her, no reproach, no sarcasm in her silent eyes.

Bathed in a unique sense of piety and glowing with the beauty and purity of heart, Pattamahishi Maharani Prabhavati glanced at Padmini. A feeble, limpid smile flowed languidly over her lips. Her liquid eyes were thoughtful and compassionate.

All hard feelings towards Padmini were washed away. Relieved, Padmini too felt released of her repressed displeasure. Suddenly, she wondered what it was all about. Why was I so needlessly apprehensive about Maharani Prabhavati's attitude towards me? This world and its maya.

Padmini silently paid her respects to the maharani.

* * *

Unaffected by the tumult of the outside world, the chanting of the sacred verses of the scriptures had begun.

'*Mrityormukshiya māmritāt.*'

The resonance of the mantras began to transform the atmosphere. The unbroken and unsubdued sound of the chanting began to rise, encircling all the women with their feelings of happiness and unhappiness, victory and defeat, joy and grief.

Fragrant wisps of smoke rose into the air.

With that, the ritual began.

The priests sprinkled a libation of water on the ground and invoked the deities. Prayers were said to invoke the divine powers, asking the benignant stars to protect them and the malignant stars to look at them kindly. *Doorvadal,* the grass, was laid near the altar. On it were offered akshat, unbroken grains of rice, petals of flowers and other articles of worship.

Pyres with logs of sandalwood were lit. A fragrance spread. Smoke from the pyres rose higher.

The exclamation of *'swaha'* while offering oblations to the gods reached far and wide, filling everybody with spiritual strength.

It was the celebration of a great sacrifice leading to mukti, liberation beyond the realm of birth and death.

Ecstasy descended from the corners of Padmini's eyes. A smile conveying a sense of detachment sat on her closed lips. Suddenly, she went back to her childhood. She distinctly remembered the day, when in a room in Tamragarh a renowned astrologer had prophesied that she would perform a great religious ritual. On that day, destiny must have smirked at the irony of his astrological calculation.

The ritual has been performed as predicted by you, Acharya, but who could have imagined then that it would be so ill-fated!

The moments from the past that had come alive were back to where they belonged. Her serene expression remained unchanged.

Time was passing by quickly. The great void continued to expand.

The time of departure for an eternal journey had come. Everyone sets out on this journey, carrying with them the baggage of their past, with nothing on their mind. During this journey, they are both together and isolated at the same time. What binds them together is the same strain of music that permeates the horizon: music that has not been played on an instrument, has not been sung by a singer, is not based on predetermined notes. Just an echo that is felt and not heard. Freed from the snare of the inanimate world, the wayfarer of this glorious journey, the illustrious queen, would not look back. She moved on towards her destination—eternity.

With each step she took, the earth seemed to cave in. The sound of eternal salvation seemed to resonate.

The huge arched gate was closer. It was a propitious moment in which her heart, her mind, her soul had become pure.

It was a moment of life meeting death.

Padmini looked at the warriors with compassion in her eyes. Standing like statues, they held unsheathed swords. They looked as though they were bearing the weight of a huge rock. They were dignified in their demeanour, but the glow of hope was missing on their faces.

She stepped forward to sit on the pyre. There was no trace of sorrow on her face. She did not seem to have any attachment to the material world and all its luxuries. There was an extraordinary gleam of triumph in her eyes. Calmly, she sat on the pyre.

Her eyes were fixed on the tip of her nose. She stopped breathing. She appeared to be taking the agni samadhi, meditating in the lap of the leaping flames. More firewood was thrown in. With the ghee being poured in, the flames rose higher and higher.

Her delicate, beautiful body became one with the fire. Flames from the burning pyre leapt ferociously. The chanting of the mantras became louder: '*mrityu jayati dhruvam . . .*'

The fire that purified her was, in turn, getting cleansed. The golden ruddy glow of dawn burst through it.

* * *

The bodies were burnt to ashes. They were freed from the bonds of worldly existence. The souls were finally emancipated.

Transcending the barriers of time and space, the liberated souls had left for their final destination.

The *purnahuti,* the offering of the final oblation, was complete.

The sun sank behind the Aravalis. Clouds of smoke rose and dispersed quietly. The darkness began to deepen. Some sparks flying off the smouldering pyres glinted in the dark.

A whole time span had been reduced to ashes and had merged into space.

Suddenly, the wind began to howl. And then, a gust swept the ashes away.